Nick's head ca...

'What's the temperat...

'Just coming.' Melanie snapped the probe onto the electronic thermometer and placed it with skilful precision into the patient's ear. The readout was instantaneous.

Nick half smiled. 'Great little gadgets, aren't they?'

'Worth every bush dance I've suffered through to raise the money for this one,' she agreed drily. 'Do you dance, Dr Cavallo?' she couldn't resist asking innocently.

'You'll just have to wait and see, won't you, Sister?'

Dear Reader

It was excitement with a capital E when I learned
A COUNTRY CALLING would be published.
Melanie and Nick leapt into my life so forcefully, I just
had to tell their story.

I live in semi-rural Queensland with my husband, Peter.
Our children have grown up and left the nest, making
family gatherings when they happen very special indeed.

Enjoy my world!

Leah Martyn

A COUNTRY CALLING

BY
LEAH MARTYN

MILLS & BOON®

For Claire, who shared her specialist
knowledge so generously. And for
my family, my true believers.

*First published in Great Britain 1999
Harlequin Mills & Boon Limited,
Eton House, 18-24 Paradise Road, Richmond, Surrey TW9 1SR*

© Leah Martyn 1999

ISBN 0 263 81421 1

*Set in Times Roman 11 on 12 pt.
03-9902-41685-D*

*Printed and bound in Norway
by AIT Trondheim AS, Trondheim*

CHAPTER ONE

MELANIE hit the floor running.

Their holiday was over. And now it's back to the real world, she thought ruefully, padding along the hall to her friend's bedroom.

Lord, it was freezing! She pulled her robe tighter and rapped on the door.

'Tam, get a move on! You're giving me a lift to work, OK?'

Something muffled and probably unrepeatable came from the other side of the door and Melanie grinned. Given half a chance, Tam would happily wallow in·warmth until midday.

Thirty minutes later they were ready to leave—two highly qualified young women, their work roles special within Murrajong District Hospital.

'Mondays in Theatre are the pits,' Tam grumbled. She looked cautiously both ways and eased her sporty Holden Barina out onto the Queensland country highway.

'All elective stuff. Visiting specialists, being picky all over the shop.'

Melanie had heard it all before. 'You love your job, Tam. And spare a thought for me. I have to try to rub along with the new relieving registrar.'

'Oh, yes.' Tam's response rippled with speculation. 'So, on the Richter scale, how did you rate him?'

Melanie's heart unaccountably thumped. 'I spoke to him for five minutes at a staff meeting before I went on leave. I hardly had time to form any impression.'

Not quite true... Despite the fact they'd spoken only briefly, every husky intonation of his voice had travelled with her throughout her two weeks away.

'Apparently, he's come from a staff post at St David's in Brisbane.'

'Odd career move.' Tam was blunt. 'From the over-funded private sector to a struggling bush hospital. What's his story?'

'I don't know that there is one.' Melanie battled with her doubts. 'He must be well qualified. I can't imagine Bryce Tierney letting his job go to just anyone, can you?'

'Probably not.' Tam shrugged. 'All that's for some dreary committee, anyway. Maybe your man's here for a stress-breaker?'

'In A and E? Hardly!'

'Hmm...' Tam tapped her fingers on the steering-wheel. 'Broken love affair, perhaps? Oh, Mel...' She looked stricken. 'That wasn't too bright of me.'

'It's OK.' Melanie gave a cracked laugh. 'You're only speaking the truth. A messed-up relationship was the reason *I* came here, after all.'

Tam flashed her friend a sharp look. 'I'm proud of you, you know. It can't have been easy, getting back into circulation, after what Aaron did to you.'

Well, she was trying, Melanie thought. Lord, how

she was trying. 'The holiday was fun, Tam. And I'm glad you talked me into it.'

'Well, don't get complacent now,' Tam warned, thumping her horn at a passing small wallaby that looked poised to change tack and leap in front of them. 'Who knows?' She grinned wickedly. 'Maybe you'll connect with the new reg.?'

Melanie felt a stab of panic. 'I'm not ready for anything like that, Tam.' A light holiday romance was one thing. But anything else...

'What name does our new man go by?' Tam asked, turning neatly into the hospital car park. 'You never did tell me.'

'Nick Cavallo,' Melanie said carefully. 'Dominic, actually, but apparently he prefers Nick.'

'Or sir.' Tam snickered and began to look for a vacant space.

'He's here!' Melanie felt a strange little dip in her stomach. The registrar's car was prestigiously obvious outside the A and E department.

Tam whistled. 'The Jag XJ? Way to go... Beats Bryce's station wagon.'

'Nick Cavallo doesn't have a wife and four kids to ferry around,' Melanie pointed out dryly. 'Tam, there's a space.'

Melanie slipped into the hospital by a side entrance. She was the charge sister in the accident and emergency department and on a permanent early shift. Her stomach was swirling with first-day-back nerves. She would have to give it her best shot. Forge some kind of decent working relationship with Nick Cavallo. She just hoped he'd meet her halfway.

She ducked into the ladies to recheck her appearance. Her fair hair, which had a tendency to be full and a bit wayward, was still in its loose knot. And while the pale blue uniform was hardly high fashion, she filled it quite nicely. And who actually cared? she thought a bit ruefully. Her gaze dropped to her watch, and her green eyes widened. It was time to take the report from the night sister.

'Sounds like you had a rough one,' Melanie commiserated with her colleague, Linda Scott.

'Tell me about it.' Linda sighed, plonking herself down on the nearest chair. 'These pile-ups terrify me.'

'Spinal case gone?' Melanie encouraged Linda's obvious need to unwind.

'The Medivac chopper was here at first light to make the transfer to Brisbane. We couldn't cope with everything. Had to dig the reg. out at two a.m.'

'How is he fitting in?' Melanie threw caution to the winds and fished blatantly for information.

'I'm probably not the best person to ask.'

'Did you have a run-in with him?' Melanie reacted coolly. Clashes of temperament were always possible in the highly stressful area where they worked.

'He lost it a bit this morning,' Linda said. 'Gave us all a serve. Said we'd prioritised the accident cases poorly.'

'And had you?'

Linda's mouth turned down. 'Who knows what they're doing at two o'clock in the morning?'

Presumably, the staff of an accident and emergency facility, Melanie thought grimly. Niggling questions about Linda's capabilities surfaced in her mind. She turned away. Already her holiday break seemed light years ago.

Her phone rang and she picked it up, slotting pens into her top pocket as she listened. 'Terrific!' She muttered, replacing the handset with a snap.

'Welcome back, Sister.'

Melanie whipped round to find her two third-years, Jane Armitage and Fiona Campbell, hovering at the door. She smiled a bit grimly. 'Thanks...I think.' She beckoned them in. 'If either of you is good at praying, now's the time. Admin's just rung. Our two ENs have called in sick.'

'Both of them!' the students said in disbelief.

'I know, I know.' Melanie blew out her breath in a sigh of resignation. 'We'll just have to manage. I'll get on to the supervisor, at least try for replacements.'

'Morning, all.' Sean Casey, one of A and E's junior resident doctors, breezed in. Tall and lanky, he towered over his female contemporaries.

'What's up?' He peered down into their serious faces.

'Double shifts, most likely,' Melanie said cryptically. 'Half the department's gone AWOL.'

'Tell me something I don't know.' He dismissed her reply with remarkable cheerfulness. 'Terrific tan, Mel,' he observed cheekily. 'All over, is it?'

She gave him a sugary smile. 'Fiji was brilliant. I've a horrible feeling I should've stayed there—'

'Is there a reason for this teaparty?'

All heads turned as one.

Melanie saw her hopes for a quiet life scatter like leaves in the wind. Cavallo was going to make waves. With folded arms, he leaned casually against the doorframe.

Her stomach dived. This is all I need, she thought, six feet plus of brooding masculinity! And then her kinder self relented. The man was obviously bone-weary. His olive complexion showed he was missing sleep. There were charcoal shadows around his eyes, deep vertical furrows in either cheek.

'Melanie.' He broke the throbbing silence and inclined his dark head curtly. 'Nice to see you back.'

'Dr Cavallo.' Her greeting was deliberately formal.

His blue eyes widened by a fraction, before returning to see-all, reveal-nothing watchfulness. 'Could we have a word in my office, please? Now.'

Melanie's hackles rose. They'd probably have several if he was going to play the heavy. For heaven's sake! she lectured herself, settling her mobile mouth into a tight line. You're twenty-eight, Melanie, just deal with it—with him.

'I have a staffing problem to sort out first. I'll be with you as soon as I can.'

'Put a rush on it, then, will you? We're supposed to be running a hospital here.' He spun away only to wheel back a pace. 'By the way, the drugs cupboard looks like a bomb hit it. See to it, would you?'

Watching his retreating back, Melanie fancied she'd just survived several horrific lifetimes.

'I'm out of here.' Sean peeled his length away from the wall and beat a hasty retreat.

'Me, too.' Linda muttered something about all work and no play and then she also made a hurried exit.

'Right, you two, we've work to do.' Melanie rounded with brisk precision on her junior nurses, deciding that the sooner she started pulling things back to something like normal the better.

'Jane, would you be responsible for triage for the moment, please?

'And, Fiona.' She turned to the willowy blond. 'Do a round of the cubicles, please. Check we've enough IV fluids. I may need to put in an order to the super. And make sure the laundry's sent us our linen and plenty of sheepskins. This cold snap is bound to trigger some early admissions from the nursing home.'

'Yes, Sister. And the drugs cupboard?' The third-year hovered uncertainly.

Melanie's mouth tightened. 'Give me a few minutes to make a couple of phone calls and we'll do it together.'

And let this be the last time Nick Cavallo will find anything to fault, she vowed silently.

From the open window of his office Nick Cavallo looked across at the paddocks, newly ploughed ready for spring planting. The turned-over soil was set out in neat patches, rather like a draughtboard, he decided with a touch of wryness, and wished his own life was as neat around the edges.

He sighed and dragged his hands through his hair,

locking them at the back of his neck. He hadn't meant to jump on the team like that.

'Fool!' he muttered, grimacing with self-derision. Obviously he'd lost the art of light-hearted hospital banter. Lord, it was what kept everyone going. And he couldn't afford to be offside with the staff. They could make his stay here quite untenable if they decided to close ranks...

A tight little smile drifted around his mouth. He certainly hadn't expected Melanie Stewart's reaction. Quick off the mark, that lady... He let his breath go in a long hiss and turned abruptly to find her standing there, her hand raised to knock.

'Hi—you wanted a word?'

Melanie saw him quickly school his expression but not before she'd read his body language. He was as moody as hell, she decided, his thoughts someplace else...or with someone else...

'Sit down,' he ordered softly.

'Sorry—?' She found herself mesmerised by the shape of his bottom lip.

'In the chair.'

She felt disorientated. She'd been in this office countless times but today it felt like alien territory. And where on earth was Bryce's familiar clutter? And was Cavallo making a fashion statement with his clothes? Melanie decided to be picky. The dark burgundy shirt and narrow black tie looked more in keeping with an upmarket men's boutique.

'So, what's the state of play?' He shrugged into a freshly laundered white coat and turned back the sleeves. 'I've got out of the way of wearing this clobber,' he said ruefully, dropping his long length into a chair.

Melanie thought of a dozen questions she could have asked about that but didn't. Instead, she flicked her eyes towards him and then away.

'I'd just like to say that what you saw in my office earlier was not what it seemed. My staff on this shift are extremely conscientious.'

'Did I say they weren't?' he observed quietly.

'You implied it.'

'Oh, don't be so bloody difficult,' he said quite mildly.

'I've never been accused of being difficult,' she denied stonily.

'OK. My apologies, then. You were standing up for your team. Speaking of which, I understand we're down on numbers.'

Melanie could have hit him with something from his expensive desk set! She swallowed.

'Sister?'

'Yes, we're critically short of staff,' she confirmed. 'Winter ills mostly. I've rung the supervisor. She'll try to find replacements.'

'Are you that philosophical?'

She shrugged and saw a flicker of irritation cross his face. Tough.

'Craig Hamilton's off too,' Nick said, referring to A and E's other resident doctor. 'Got this flu bug. Have you had your shots?'

'Of course.'

His gaze narrowed, probed. 'Anything else on the agenda?'

Melanie held his gaze—just. 'We've had an emergency call.' Gathering her wits, she began to fill him in.

'The patient is a twenty-year-old male, name of Steven Fraser. He works for a sawmill. I've spoken to their foreman. It's a hand injury.'

Nick pursed his lips. 'Can we expect arterial damage?'

'He says not. Bones possibly broken and lacerations to his forearm.'

'I see.' He lifted a hand and traced a thoughtful pattern across his chin. 'Did you manage to find out what kind of machinery was being used? It might give us a clue to the tissue damage.'

'A docking saw,' Melanie supplied shortly. 'Apparently, it jammed.'

'Ambulance bringing him in?'

She nodded. 'But they've a way to come. The mill's at Linville.'

Nick slewed around in his chair, one arm sliding over its back. 'I'm the new chum around here. How far out of town is that?'

'Oh...twenty, twenty-five kilometres.'

He acknowledged the information with one of his curt nods. 'Thank you, Sister. You've been very thorough. But, then, I suspect you always are.'

Melanie made straight for the sanctuary of her office, side-stepping the cleaners with practised ease, although her composure was shot to pieces. Her mind was reeling. Where did he get off, making that barbed little comment? For heaven's sake! It was her job to be thorough!

She'd hardly had time to pull her thoughts together when the low wail of the ambulance echoed around the rear entrance of the hospital. Hurrying towards the receiving bay, she collected Jane along the way.

'Oh— Dr Cavallo's already waiting.' Jane fell back a pace.

Melanie's legs suddenly felt like lead. He acknowledged her with a crooked smile, and her chin came up. She hoped he got the message.

The ambulance slid to a halt and Bob Brand, the senior officer, sprang lightly from the rear of the vehicle. 'Morning, folks. Early customer for you.'

'Any problems on the way in, Bob?' Nick moved to take a share of the weight and the injured youth was transferred gently to the hospital trolley.

'BP took a nose dive about a mile back, Doc.'

Melanie exchanged glances with the registrar. The boy looked very shocked.

'Let's move it.' Nick's voice was clipped.

'Cubicle two's ready.' Melanie's response was crisply calm and suddenly, miraculously, they were working as a well-oiled team, their earlier differences smoothed away.

'Lift the space blanket, please, Jane.' Melanie bent to take the boy's blood pressure.

'You're going around his thigh?' The student registered surprise and Melanie nodded.

'Eighty-five on fifty.' She released the cuff.

'Pulse isn't brilliant either,' Nick muttered, easing off the thick gauze pad covering the boy's injured hand. His mouth tightened. Poor bloody kid. There were certainly broken bones and major soft tissue damage—a hunting ground for infection. The tiny fragments of sawdust were a killer, embedded into the wound—probably right into the bone-ends. What a mess.

Nick's head came up interrogatively. 'What's the temperature reading, Sister?'

'Just coming.' Melanie snapped the probe onto the electronic thermometer and placed it with skilful precision into Steven Fraser's ear. The readout was instantaneous. 'Thirty-five point five,' she said, her eyes moving involuntarily to the registrar's.

He half smiled. 'Great little gadgets, aren't they?'

'Worth every bush dance I've suffered through to raise the money for this one,' she agreed drily. 'Do you dance, Dr Cavallo?' she couldn't resist asking innocently.

The firm lips gave a cool imitation of a smile. 'You'll just have to wait and see, won't you, Sister? Now, let's get an IV in here, please. Eighteen gauge cannula.'

'Beside you on the bench.' Melanie slipped straight back into professional mode. 'What drugs do you need?'

'Better make it fifty milligrams of pethidine. He's in some pain here.'

'Maxolon?' Melanie queried, as Steven Fraser began to retch miserably.

'Ten milligrams,' Nick confirmed, and directed the boy's head towards the basin.

Melanie snatched up the keys to the drugs cupboard and detailed Jane to accompany her. In another few months Jane herself would be qualified and a preceptor to her own junior.

The third-year said wryly, 'I've watched you do this a thousand times, Sister.'

'Then watch a thousand and one,' Melanie replied evenly. 'That way you won't get sued for giving the wrong medication.'

Following hospital procedure, they went on to double-check Nick's scrawled instructions and then took a precautionary look at the injured boy's wrist. There was no Alert bracelet. Melanie bent over him and asked gently, 'Are you allergic to any drugs, Steven?'

'D-don't think so...'

She injected the painkiller and antiemetic.

Shortly afterwards Jane was despatched with blood for cross-matching and Melanie breathed a sigh of relief. The medication and saline drip were starting to do their work.

She stepped quietly into an adjoining cubbyhole, where Nick was examining the injured youth's X-rays. 'Steven's pinking up nicely,' she said, satisfaction in the guarded smile she gave him.

'Advantages of being young and otherwise in good shape,' he reflected, peering intently at the images on the screen. 'He's in for a long old op, I'm afraid. That hand is going to need a compound scrub if he's to regain full mobility.'

'Just as well we have a visiting hand man on duty today, then,' Melanie said, 'otherwise we'd have had to send him on.'

Nick opened his mouth and then clamped it shut.

It was frustrating him like hell not to have the free-
dom to follow his patients through to Theatre and
finish the job. His hollow laugh stayed locked in his
throat. He had to keep reminding himself he'd taken
this relieving post at the direction of his heart—not
his head.

He rounded on Melanie, his blue eyes very intense. 'Just who the hell owns this sawmill?'

Startled, she took a step back. 'I have no idea.
Does it matter?'

'Of course it *matters*!' He gave scathing emphasis
to the final word. 'Injuries like this don't just happen.
Not if machinery is kept properly maintained.'

Well, what did he expect her to do? Melanie
fumed. Go racing out to Linville with an army of
government safety inspectors?

She glanced at him, disconcerted to see him slowly
roll back his shoulders as if to relieve an aching
tiredness. Which probably accounted for his foul
mood earlier, she decided. 'Did you manage any
sleep at all after the RTA call-out?'

'I'll live,' he grunted.

Her mouth thinned. 'No doubt you will. But you
must be out on your feet.'

He gave an impatient twitch of his shoulder. 'If I
find myself nodding off, I'll jump under a cold
shower.'

Melanie's breath spun out on a tight little sigh. She
shouldn't have started this. 'Working here has got to
be light years away from what you're used to.'

He gave a snort of laughter. 'How do you know
what I'm used to?'

'I don't—' She swallowed unevenly. 'Forget I spoke.' Let him keep his damned secrets! Trying to communicate with him was like negotiating a mine-field—blindfolded.

She gave it one last shot. 'If you feel like crashing out later, there's a kind of communal couch in my office.'

His eyebrows rose. 'And what should I deduce from that, exactly?'

The inexplicable resentment she'd been tamping down ever since they'd met that morning rose to the surface irretrievably. 'You know perfectly well.'

'I don't need you to *nurture* me, Sister.' He made the word sound almost indecent and Melanie froze. Did he imagine she was coming on to him?

'In your dreams!'

Nick responded with a knowing smile, one that had tiny goosebumps breaking out all over her. Oh, Lord.

'Excuse me...' Fiona appeared like a tall guardian angel in the doorway. 'Steven's mum's here.' She looked curiously from the charge to the registrar. 'What shall I tell her?'

Nick was the first to recover himself. 'I'll speak with her,' he said shortly, thrusting the X-rays at Melanie. 'See these get to Theatre with him, please.'

Shaken, Melanie stared at his departing back. He'd left in his wake a whole chain reaction of emotions that frightened the life out of her. With painstaking care she'd spent the past months weaving a safety net around her innermost feelings. Now she needed fresh air. Great lungsful of it.

'Penny for them.' RN Suzy Parker stuck her head with its wild tangle of red curls around the door.

Melanie recovered herself quickly. 'Oh... Hi, Suz. What can I do for you?'

'It's more what I can do for you,' the other said cheerfully. 'I've been pooled to you, ducky.'

'Oh, great! Not busy in Gynae?'

Suzy pulled a face. 'Our five little beds all pristine and empty. Want me to take over here?'

'Would you?' Melanie said gratefully. 'I do have something I should chase up.'

'Or someone,' Suzy quipped. 'Saw your new reg. outside. Is he hot or what...!'

'If you go for tall, dark, bloody-minded men,' Melanie qualified stiffly.

'Uh-oh.' Suzy laughed softly. 'Like that, is it?' She picked up Steven Fraser's chart, scanning it with a professional eye. 'Maybe you should try loosening his tie, Mel. You never know what might happen.'

'I should get so close!' Melanie snorted.

'Should you?'

Suzie's grin was wicked and Melanie blushed. She bit her lip. Perhaps her emotional *glue* wasn't holding as well as she'd thought. 'Suz, don't...' she pleaded softly. 'I've had a hell of a morning.'

'Chuck me an apron, then.' Suzy's mirth still lingered. 'Sponge and prep our young man for Theatre, right?'

'Please. Jane should be back shortly to give you a hand. And Theatre asked if someone from here could take him up. They're flat out with elective surgery today.'

'You've got it,' Suzy complied cheerfully, proceeding to wrap her small person in an oversized plastic apron.

Melanie was barely halfway back to her office when Fiona claimed her attention. 'There's a patient asking personally for you,' the third-year said doubtfully. 'I've put her in cubicle four.'

'Thanks, Fi.' Melanie twitched aside the curtains on the cubicle and went in.

'Evie!' She smiled in recognition and moved across to the treatment couch where Fiona had settled the elderly patient.

'Oh... Melanie, dear.' Evie Dean's pale eyes fluttered behind her spectacles and she managed a faint smile. 'I was so afraid you were still on holidays.'

'Just back today.' Melanie took the thin hand and held it. 'What have you done to yourself? Is it the leg again?'

The old lady's chest rose and fell in a shaky sigh. 'I'm afraid so. I bumped it, you see, and it bled quite a bit.'

Melanie patted her hand. 'Well, let's just have a look at it.' Deftly, she stripped away the tired old crêpe bandage.

The varicose vein was dilated but Evie's leg showed no significant swelling. Melanie looked thoughtful. The old lady had an inborn weakness in the walls of her vein but, provided she took proper care, the condition might never worsen.

'I hope I'm not being a nuisance.' Evie clasped her thin hands across her chest. 'I thought Dr Tierney should check it...'

'You did the right thing,' Melanie said, and gave her patient a reassuring smile. 'But you'll have to see one of the other doctors this time. Dr Tierney's on three months' leave. Just relax now. We'll have you sorted out in no time.'

Where are you, Sean? Melanie cast a slightly desperate search up and down the casualty area.

'Can I help?'

She spun around. Nick Cavallo stood like a second shadow behind her.

'I hope so,' she said stiffly, and began to fill him in about Evie Dean's condition.

'Primary varicosities is hardly an emergency,' he pointed out logically. 'Surely it's a matter for her GP?'

'She doesn't have one.' Melanie gritted her teeth. Why did she have to justify everything to him? 'Mrs Dean has always come here for treatment. A lot of our elderly folk do. They appreciate contact with the staff. And you don't approve,' she pre-empted bluntly, seeing his mouth pull down at the corners.

'We can't have them using Casualty as a kind of club,' Nick said calmly.

'So, are you proposing changing our policy, then?'

Her green eyes snapped at him and Nick studied her. Did she feel so passionately about *everything*? he wondered. His mouth hardened. 'Nothing so extreme, Sister. But while we're short on staff, I'd prefer you to aim the non-urgent cases towards one or other of the GPs.'

Melanie felt like hitting him. Only a professional control allowed her to meet his gaze without showing any of the helplessness that clamped her stomach at the needless hurt and upset his arrogant decision could let loose on these old folk.

She tossed the initiative right back to him. 'Do you wish me to inform Mrs Dean you're not about to treat her, then?'

He stared at her as though she needed a brain scan. 'There's no need to go that far. Of course I'll see her.'

Melanie heaved in a breath sharp with bitterness.

'Cubicle four,' she said abruptly, and followed him in, standing protectively beside Evie as he examined her. He was thorough. She had to give him that. And even if his questions to the old lady were direct, they were nothing but kind and interested. Had she expected anything less of him? Melanie felt a nebulous kind of shame engulf her, when she realised she had.

Having completed his examination, Nick leaned both hands on the bed beside his patient. 'How did this last episode happen, Mrs Dean? Did you fall?'

Evie's pale eyes behind her spectacles opened, wide and innocent. 'I got tangled up with Mendelssohn.'

'Dare I ask?'

Nick's dry plea for enlightenment tipped Melanie's mouth into a guarded smile.

'Mendelssohn is a cat. A huge, great tabby, isn't he, Evie?'

'Yes, dear. He certainly is,' the old lady agreed. 'And bossy and overbearing. But I'd miss him if he wasn't there.'

Nick looked thoughtful as he left the bedside and went to the washbasin in the corner. 'We could get the healing process under way much more quickly if you'd come and spend a few days in hospital with us,' he threw over his shoulder.

There was a puckering of Evie's brow as she assimilated this. 'I would rather, not, thank you all the same, Doctor.'

'Well, that's entirely up to you, of course.' His expression was unreadable and he folded his arms and looked down at his elderly patient. 'Meanwhile, I suggest you invest in some elasticated support hose. If you can't obtain them locally, I'm sure the hospital dispensary would order them in for you.' He turned pointedly to Melanie. 'I'd like Mrs Dean's leg bandaged now, please, Sister. And do you think we could run to a cup of tea for her?'

Melanie stared at him as if he'd gone mad. It seemed that once he'd started he couldn't stop! 'I'm sure we could, Doctor,' she answered automatically, suddenly finding his presence adding a vulnerability to her already strained emotions.

'Back in a minute.' She directed a taut little smile at Evie and followed the registrar outside.

'Don't look so surprised.' Frustration at her silent, judgemental scrutiny of his patient skills had goaded Nick into mocking retribution. He swore silently. She may as well have been holding a knife between his shoulder blades!

'I'm not!' she said defensively in an angry undertone.

'Bull! You had me pegged as a monster.'

Had she? Melanie swallowed thickly. 'You were very kind to Evie. Thank you.'

'Part of the job, I would have thought.' Nick heard his reply, curt and dismissive, and winced inwardly. For crying out loud, they were both supposed to be on the same side of this equation, not trying to out-score one another.

He smiled a bit grimly. 'Evie Dean seems a gutsy little lady, but I gathered the impression she battles on alone. Does she have family here?'

'She doesn't, actually.' Melanie felt herself soft-ening. 'Two sons, both married and living interstate.'

'Has she been put in touch with the social worker in case things start going wrong?'

'Not to my knowledge.'

'Then I think we should organise it as soon as possible.'

Melanie flared briefly. Evie would hate the intru-sion into her privacy and independence. 'She really manages quite well.' Melanie didn't add that she her-self called in on Evie at least weekly.

'For now.' The dark head turned sharply in her direction. 'Would you have a chat with the social worker? Today, if you can manage it?'

Melanie caught at her lower lip. 'Robyn is not in today. The job is funded for only twenty hours a week. She normally works from Tuesday to Friday.' Now he'll probably hold me responsible for the va-garies of Health Department funding, she thought darkly.

But he didn't.

Instead, he laughed a bit hollowly. 'Why do I get the impression I'm being re-educated around here?'

His blue eyes burned into hers, as if seeking an answer, then unaccountably broke the contact to move slowly, deliberately, across her face and down her throat to where the V of her collar ended.

'Call me if you need me.' With that, he about-turned and left her standing there.

Melanie watched his long-limbed stride, her hand fluttering up to the bare skin of her throat as if to shield it. Her mind raced in ridiculous circles, starting, recycling and going nowhere, until finally she managed to force a stop to the process.

She shook her head as if to clear it. She and Nick Cavallo were just going through the usual settling-in period, she told herself decisively, dismissing the frisson of sensation that crept, light-fingered, along her spine as her own vivid imagination.

CHAPTER TWO

'WHAT you need, girl, is to get back to routine.'

Melanie passed judgement on her fuzzy thinking in the only way she knew how. Glancing at her watch, she frowned. They had spent an inordinate amount of time with Evie. Could she have been just as well served by a visit to a GP? Was Nick Cavallo right? The fact that he might have been set her teeth on edge.

With quiet efficiency, she delegated Evie's care to Jane and then began to check what other casualties they'd managed to collect so far that Monday.

She found Bill Tyler, a council worker, waiting for an eye wash. She settled him in the small treatment room.

'I'll do Mr Tyler,' she told Suzy, who was on the run from another section.

'Oh, good.' The red-headed nurse held tightly to the kidney dish she was carrying. 'I can't get back to him for a while. The poor guy copped a load of sand and grit in the eye when the lads were unloading turf for the new sports oval. Eye looks painful,' she grimaced.

'He'll probably need a medical certificate for time off work,' Melanie said consideringly. 'Sean about for a signature?'

'Suturing. Little kid fell, getting out of the school bus. Put a great gash in her knee.'

'Parents alerted?'

'Dad's just arrived.' Suzy craned her neck towards Reception. 'Is Nick about? I need him to look at my patient.'

Melanie bit the underside of her lip. 'Staffroom, I think. What's up?'

Suzy made a small moue. 'Young teenager overdosed on her mum's sleeping pills, then panicked. I've just had the pleasure of cleaning her up.'

'Cry for help?' Melanie's eyes widened quizzically.

'Probably.' Suzy shrugged. 'In over her head with some guy, apparently. No one to talk to. Mum's busy with her own boyfriend. Same old story.'

'Oh, for a psych unit.' Melanie sighed.

'May as well wish for Lotto. Ah—there's Nick now.'

'I hear you've been playing mud pies, Bill.' Melanie addressed her patient cheerfully, as she donned gloves and bent to examine the injured eye.

'Silly bloody kid! Sorry, Sister,' he apologised awkwardly, 'but it hurts like the devil.'

'I can believe that.' Melanie began the wash-out immediately. 'Your eye has suffered quite some trauma.' Slowly and methodically she cleansed the eye and gently swabbed one last time. 'That's it, Bill. Sorry if it was painful for you.'

'It's OK, love. Thanks,' he responded gruffly. 'I'd like to blow my nose, though.'

'Sure.' Melanie helped him into a sitting position and handed him a large box of tissues. 'Stay there for a minute,' she insisted, touching a hand to his shoulder. 'I'll get one of the doctors to write you a certificate for the time you'll be off work.'

The big man looked at her in mystification. 'Lloyd's outside, waiting for me.'

'Lloyd?' Melanie's eyebrows rose fractionally.

'Lloyd Beaumann, the foreman.' Bill Tyler looked ill at ease, obviously not wanting to go against hospital policy but just as obviously feeling obliged to get back to his job as soon as possible. 'I'm not sick, love,' he remonstrated uncomfortably.

Melanie schooled her expression into the mode of officialdom. 'I'm afraid I must ask you to wait until a doctor has seen you, Bill. He may decide you'll need eyedrops and in that case you'll need a script, won't you?'

The big man reddened, interlocking his work-worn hands. 'I s'pose so.'

Hiding a smile, Melanie left him to contemplate his feet, clad in their thick, black work socks, swinging free off the edge of the treatment couch.

Allowing her smile full reign, she pushed through the swing doors of the treatment room. Too late she realised her dilemma. She had nowhere to go but straight into Nick Cavallo's broad expanse of chest.

'Oh! Sorry!' she apologised breathlessly, pulling her nose away from the front of his shirt where she'd connected—but not before she'd caught the tang of a woodsy cologne.

'OK?' Nick's hands had flown up automatically to

steady her, and now he was looking enquiringly into her flushed face.

'Fine, thanks...'

His hands dropped. 'Did you want me?'

For a split second Melanie's heart cartwheeled. She avoided answering, drawing him instead into a just-vacated cubicle. She filled him in quickly.

Nick's pose was relaxed as he leaned against the wall, looking at her. 'So, you want me to play the heavy?'

You do it so well, she wanted to say, but resisted the temptation. It really wouldn't be fair. Not now. She'd got the impression he was trying like mad to paper over the very scratchy start they'd made to their professional relationship.

She forced out a brief smile. 'Would you mind? Should be a piece of cake for you, anyway.'

Nick looked pensive. 'In what way?'

Melanie shrugged. 'Patients of the calibre of Bill Tyler take your word for gospel.'

'Because I'm a doctor?'

'No.' Melanie gave a small, impatient tut. 'Because you're a male!'

'Ah!' His lips twisted into a thoughtful moue. 'Interesting theory. Let's see if it has legs, shall we?'

In the space of a few minutes Bill Tyler was reassured, briefly counselled and provided with a medical certificate and prescription.

'These drops contain an antibiotic, Bill,' the registrar cautioned. 'Use them for three days only. Then, if you're at all concerned about your eye, come back and see us.'

'Sure thing, Doc. Thanks.' Bill Tyler lowered his big frame to the floor and worked his feet back into his elastic-sided work boots. Standing with his feet apart, he eyed the new doctor and the slender, fair-haired sister beside him. 'I'll get the script filled and then Lloyd can run me home.' He grinned disarmingly as he left. 'Can't remember when I last had any sick days.'

'Well, he looked pretty pleased with himself.' Moving with quiet efficiency, Melanie began to put the treatment room back in order.

Nick chuckled. 'I was tempted to lay the whole working-in-the-sun bit on him as well.'

'Oh, I think our outdoor workers are educated enough these days to wear sun-screen and protective clothing,' she said.

'And shades?' Nick made huge circles around his eyes with his thumb and forefinger. 'Hundred per cent UV protection?'

Melanie's mouth went up in a wry little twist. 'In Murrajong? Well…maybe not.' Deftly, she slid a fresh sheet on the treatment couch. A few quick, decisive twists and it was done. She turned to Nick, her hand on the neat, tucked-in end, not believing how far they'd come.

'Coffee?' It was a single word but to Nick it spoke volumes. What wondrously compassionate eyes she had. The observation came a bit disjointedly, took him unawares.

'Make it tea and you've got a deal.' He cleared his throat as an inner warning light flashed, and clamped down on the strangeness of his feelings.

'I'll bring it in to you,' she offered. Despite his protestations, he really did looked bushed.

'Hmm? Oh, thanks. I'd appreciate it.' He smiled a bit grimly. 'I'd better start a ring-around for a locum.'

Melanie frowned. 'Craig's that sick?'

'Sick enough,' Nick confirmed. 'I've advised him to take a period of R and R tacked onto his sick leave.'

'Good luck, then.' He'd need it, Melanie thought wryly. In her experience, locum doctors these days were reluctant to venture more than fifty miles away from a major city and Murrajong was at least three hours' drive from Brisbane, which might daunt a prospective locum. Yet for some reason it obviously hadn't daunted Nick Cavallo...

In the staffroom Melanie found Sean, contemplating the dregs of a carton of chocolate-flavoured milk.

'Energy hit,' he grinned, draining the contents and then aiming the carton with deadly accuracy towards the bin. 'Bit of a scatter among the pigeons this morning, eh?'

There was no need to guess to what he was referring, but Melanie had no desire to discuss Nick Cavallo's censure with Sean or anyone else. 'The place *was* a tip, actually,' she stated calmly.

Sean tried disarming her with one of his lopsided grins. 'You didn't have to wear it, Mel. The night shift was slack.'

As if she didn't know that! Privately, she'd been appalled at how the place had been left. Linda would have to shape up.

Melanie shrugged. 'Ultimately, the bucks stops with me.'

'But you'd been on leave!' he protested.

'Tough…I guess.' She didn't need Sean to stand up for her. She'd been doing it for herself since she was a child. Still, it was sweet of him. Switching on the kettle, she began to rummage for teabags.

'Tam enjoy Fiji?'

Melanie averted her gaze, not in the least surprised by Sean's abrupt change of topic. She'd begun to suspect that he fancied her friend like mad.

'Why don't you simply ask her out, Sean?'

'Am I that transparent?' He spluttered with laughter, his hands shoved deeply into his pockets, as he peered out the window. 'She'd probably laugh in my face.'

'Oh, come on, Dr Casey!' Melanie poured boiling water into the small teapot. 'You're the original Mr Cool around women.'

'Tam's a knockout,' he commented soulfully, as if that explained his reluctance.

'For heaven's sake,' Melanie expostulated. 'Use your initiative. Bump into her casually in the canteen or something.'

'I tried that.' He fiddled with the catch on the window. 'Our breaks never seem to coincide.'

'Well, you'd better pick up the phone and try her in Theatre, then.' Melanie racked her brains in desperation. 'Leave a message if she can't come to the phone. I'm sure she'll ring back.'

'Give me break, Mel! Then the whole damn place'll know if she turns me down.' Sean spoke with such sincerity that it was all Melanie could do not to laugh.

'A touch low on self-esteem today, aren't we, Doctor?' She dipped her head to hide her smile as she loaded the small tray to take to Nick. 'Anyhow,' she reflected, 'I have it on good authority a certain lady would quite welcome an invitation from a certain resident.'

'Yeah?' Sean's face split into a grin a mile wide. 'You sure?'

'Yeah.' Melanie picked up the tray and thought cryptically, I should get a matchmaker's fee for this.

'All right!' Sean punched the air and sauntered out, as if he were taking a casual stroll—on water.

The day ground on. Melanie found herself needed here, there and everywhere. 'This is ridiculous!' she fumed, slamming the phone down after another abortive attempt to secure the practical, hands-on services of an enrolled nurse for the remainder of the shift.

'Have you been to lunch?'

She swung round. The tone of Nick's voice clearly indicated he'd witnessed her frustration.

'No. No, not yet,' she said, her brain starting to go into overload at the complications her first day back on duty were bringing. 'I'll just bet the late shift's running at full complement,' she added darkly.

'You could always lower the tension and break some plates.' Nick's laugh was unexpected, a rumble of huskiness, and the sound riveted her attention and then tiptoed up her spine.

To cover her confusion, she huffed irritably. 'Did you have this kind of fiasco at St David's?'

His face suddenly lost all its vitality. 'No. At least not where I was.'

And where was that? she was tempted to ask, but didn't. It was as if a hand on her shoulder held her back, counselling her not to.

The canteen was set apart from the hospital, a long, white building with its own bit of garden. Melanie entered through the sliding glass doors and looked about her.

It was way past the normal lunch hour but there were still small groups of hospital personnel scattered throughout the dining area. Melanie recognised some theatre staff, feeling disappointed when Tam was not amongst them. Reconciled to eating on her own, she moved across to the service counter.

There wasn't a lot left to choose from. Finally, she selected a bowl of vegetable soup and a bread roll and went and sat at a table near the window. A little smile played around her mouth. Obviously, the grocery shopping would be down to her today.

Tam, bless her, had wanted to see her grandmother. The elderly Mary O'Shea doted on her eldest grandchild and was eagerly waiting to see their holiday snaps.

Melanie crumbled her bread roll, her expression faintly wistful. Tamsin was lucky. Her warm extended family all lived locally, and while her friend might complain they were inclined to be nosy from time to time Melanie knew their positive influence had made Tam the very competent and confident person she was. Whereas she—

Enough of that! She gave a fractured little sigh and got to her feet, returning her tray with a warm smile for the long-suffering kitchen staff.

Outside the air was clear and pure, a typical winter's day in south-west Queensland. Like a somnolent cat, Melanie flexed her shoulders, feeling the sun pleasantly warm on her back as she moved slowly along the timber ramp.

Her fair head came up, her eyes thoughtfully assessing the dun-gold grass of the paddocks beyond the fringe of the hospital and the dark blue-green of the eucalypts that lined the meandering path of the creek as it wound along the edge of the town.

She sighed. Murrajong had rescued her, helped her make sense of her life, but did she really belong here, she wondered, any more than Nick Cavallo did?

A muted sound of irritation left her mouth. Why on earth was she suddenly bracketing their names in her mind?

A swift glance at her fob watch told her she still had a few minutes of her allotted break, and she chose to spend them beside the winter rose garden. The splashy pinks, reds and yellows were the pride of the hospital's groundsman, Dan Nissen, and as if she'd conjured him up he rounded the corner on his rider-mower and pulled up beside her.

'I'm just admiring the roses, Dan,' Melanie said with a smile. 'They're gorgeous this year.'

'Too right, Sister.' His thin, dark face lit up with a shy grin. 'Would you like one?' He leapt off the mower, whipped out a small pair of secateurs from his back pocket and snipped off a just-opening bud. He handed it to her.

'Mmm.' Melanie touched the dark, velvety petals to her nostrils. 'It's just lovely, Dan. Thanks.'

What a nice thing to do, she thought, her step lighter as she made her way back along the path to A and E.

Hunting through a cupboard, she found a specimen vase for her rose. Such an array of colour in one tiny bloom, she marvelled, holding the folded petals up to the light. And so soft! She touched the dark red smoothness to her lips, her eyes wistful...

'Ah—Melanie! You're back!' Nick Cavallo's voice cut through her dreaming, like scissors through silk, and to her dismay she felt the vase slip from her fingers and shatter on the tiled floor.

'Did you have to come sneaking up on me like that?' She glared at the registrar, trying to ignore the wild thumping of her heart.

'Get me something to clean it up,' Nick ordered, rescuing her rose from among the debris and placing it on the bench.

'For Goodness' sake, don't cut yourself!' Melanie fluttered around him.

He glinted a blue glance at her. 'Just for the record, I didn't sneak up on you. You were away with the fairies. Well away.'

Melanie looked away quickly, feeling the heat rising from her toes upwards until she flushed almost guiltily.

'I need to talk to you about a patient,' he said,

shoving the last of the glass fragments in the bin and then turning to wash his hands. 'How's your Japanese?'

'My what?'

'Sean tells me you have knowledge of the language.'

Melanie stared at him in disbelief. 'That was ages ago.'

'But you were an exchange student there, right?'

'Yes…' Her eyes widened and she wondered what was coming next. 'Who's the patient?'

Nick's head came round, the light from the window illuminating the hard line of his jaw with its rapidly darkening growth. 'A young tourist, Kiyo Yamaguchi. She's been on a coach tour the best part of a week. Became ill this morning and the coach captain detoured here to seek medical attention for her.'

Melanie looked uncertainly at him. 'What's happened to her?'

'Miscarriage.'

'Oh.' Her throat closed, while her sympathy raced out to the young woman, thousands of miles from home and faced with the trauma of losing her baby. 'How awful for her… She must be feeling terribly vulnerable.'

Nick gave her a long look. 'It's her first baby so, yes, she's pretty emotional.'

'You'll admit her for a D and C?' Melanie felt her heart begin to pound uncomfortably.

He nodded. 'It's indicated. I'm taking her to Theatre shortly. Suzy's prepping her now.'

Their eyes met in acknowledgement of the part he wanted Melanie to play. She bit convulsively on her lower lip, her green eyes clouding with doubt.

'I don't know if I can do this, Nick. It's been years... Whatever I've retained has got to be hopelessly rusty.'

'It's got to be better than mine,' he affirmed ruefully. 'The tour guide spoke English and I was able to gather and impart information through her. But now she's zapped off with her party and I'm left with a frightened young woman who can't understand a blind bit of anything that's being said around her.'

Melanie pictured herself in the Japanese girl's place and shuddered inwardly.

Nick sent her a searching look. 'If you could be there for Kiyo when she comes back from Recovery it would be an enormous help all round. She'll need reassurance in a big way and practical help to reorganise her plans.'

'You wouldn't recommend she try to rejoin her tour?'

'Good grief, no!' Nick moved to the fridge and helped himself to a bottle of water. 'Their schedules are killing, even for the fittest—well, I guess they have to be. They're keen to see everything the country has to offer.'

'If we were in a city hospital we'd have access to an interpreter or at least a social worker with the skills to co-ordinate all this.' Melanie began to mount her excuses plaintively.

Nick's open-palmed shrug said it all.

She felt her throat thicken. He had no idea what

he was asking of her... She saw him glance at his watch. They both knew he should be scrubbing.

'All I'm asking is a few minutes of your time, Melanie.'

And the rest! She took a huge, shaky breath. If she found the right words Kiyo would be comforted. But if she messed it up...

'All right. Ask someone in Gynae to give me a ring when Kiyo is back from Recovery. I'll do what I can.'

'Thank you.' Nick dipped his dark head in acknowledgement and left quietly.

'I'll keep this short, if you don't mind,' Melanie said to her counterpart, Mike Treloar, when the late shift assembled for hand-over.

'Anxious to get out of the place, hmm?' The senior RN slid her one of his wry, crooked smiles.

'I wish! I've still to get over to Gynae and act as interpreter for a patient.' Melanie felt her heart increase its rhythm. Just saying it had made her stomach twist with nerves and apprehension.

'Is it that young Japanese girl?' Mike asked interestedly.

Melanie's mouth turned down. 'Heard about our small drama, did you?'

He chuckled. 'The whole town's heard about it. I believe both the pubs were called on at short notice to provide lunch for the coachload of tourists.'

'And did they manage?'

Mike's amusement lingered. 'I guess so. I'm sorry

about your patient, but the thing does have its funny side.'

'In what way?' Melanie asked absently, shuffling the day's notes into a neat pile.

He leaned his stocky frame against the steel filing cabinet. 'Well, nothing was pre-planned and I have this mental picture of our Japanese visitors, tackling the very basic Aussie tucker at Dooley's and the Imperial.'

Melanie drummed up a brief smile. 'I guess it would be nothing like they're used to,' she conceded, 'but then, that's half the idea of travelling to another country, isn't it?'

'Ah, Mel.' Mike patted her shoulder, his voice very kind. 'You're way too sane and sensible.'

Or had he meant humourless? Melanie sighed and looked away. He probably had and it wasn't how she normally was at all. But today...well, the sooner to-day moved on to tomorrow the better!

Melanie entered the gynae ward almost silently and stopped. 'You're still on duty!'

Suzy Parker looked up from the nurses' desk and grinned. 'Not officially.' She relaxed her arms into a slow stretch. 'I just thought Kiyo might like a familiar face when she came round. Well, a semi-familiar face,' she amended. 'Oh, roses! Aren't they gorgeous?' She jumped to her feet, burying her nose in the sweet fragrance from the huge bunch of blooms Melanie was holding.

'Fiona charmed them out of Dan Nissen.' Melanie touched her fingertips to the red, pink and buttery yellow petals. 'She thought they might cheer Kiyo up.'

'They probably will.' Suzy took the flowers carefully. 'I'll just get a vase. Are you going in to see her?' Suzy sent a brief sideways gesture towards the pale pink screens.

'How is she?' Instinctively, Melanie put her hand on her heart, unnerved to feel how it was hammering.

Suzy pursed her lips thoughtfully. 'A bit weepy. But I helped her dress in her own nightie and brushed her hair. I think she's lightened up a bit now. And Nick's just been in to have a word with her. Well, not exactly a *word*.' She reconsidered. 'Smiles and sign language mostly. He's terrific, isn't he?'

With this little gem of wisdom, Suzy ducked into a nearby utility room with the flowers, leaving Melanie to contemplate her friend's summation of Nick Cavallo's character.

A bit dazedly she walked across to the second-floor window and looked out. Her own reaction to the man was still volatile. They'd collided rather than met, but she'd be a fool to pretend they were indifferent to one another—on one level at least...

'Here we are. Don't they look fabulous? Shame we can't say they're from her husband.'

Melanie stared. 'She's married?'

'Well, yes.' Suzy's eyes widened. 'What made you think she wasn't?'

Melanie shrugged and went cold. 'No one said. I just assumed... Why wasn't he with her?'

'Search me.' Suzy wrinkled her pert nose. 'You'll have to ask her, Mel.'

'I will.' Melanie picked up the vase, so anxious her palms were sweating. 'That's if I can remember the word for husband. Wish me luck, Suz,' she implored huskily, and flicked back the pale pink screen.

Memories of some of the happiest months of her life came rushing back as her eyes met those of the Japanese girl.

Kiyo looked younger than her twenty-six years, her hair caught, child-like, in bunches and looking almost blue-black against the stark whiteness of the pillows.

Melanie took a shaken breath and managed a tentative smile as she placed the roses on the bedside cabinet.

Her heart was cartwheeling. Please, God, let me do this right, she agonised, and pulled up a chair.

CHAPTER THREE

NICK got swiftly to his feet as Melanie came from the gynae ward and into the softly lit patients' lounge. Already the afternoon had drawn in and the tearose-printed curtains had been drawn.

She stopped as if she'd been struck. 'What are you doing here?'

'Waiting for you.' He frowned. She looked shattered and, unless he was mistaken, she'd been crying.

'Why?' Her throat convulsed as she swallowed.

'I thought you might need a lift home—or do you have a car?'

Melanie looked confusedly at him, her hands bunching into the pockets of her navy-blue blazer. 'It's in dock. They're waiting for a part...'

'Then I'll give you a lift.'

Without another word passing between them, Melanie found herself being ushered through the hospital and out into the car park. Nick stopped beside the Jaguar and unlocked the passenger door. She hesitated, looking up uncertainly at him.

'Hop in,' he urged a trifle impatiently. 'It's too cold to hang about considering your options. And far too late,' she thought she heard him mutter as he went round the bonnet and unlocked the driver's side of the car. Within seconds he had them moving swiftly along the tree-lined drive.

Melanie sighed with relief, feeling the warmth from the heater circulate around her feet.

'You look like you could use a stiff brandy.' Nick cast a discerning sideways glance at her.

'A bottle more like.' Melanie's laughter was decidedly hollow.

'That bad, hmm?' A small frown appeared between his dark brows.

'No, not really.' The words came out on a sigh. 'Kiyo is a sweetie.'

'So you managed to communicate?'

Melanie bit her lip. 'Yes, after a bit of initial awkwardness we actually managed to empathise pretty well.'

'So what happened,' he asked very quietly, 'to make you look—devastated?'

'Nothing.' Melanie's gaze flickered and went still.

'Oh, come on, Melanie! I'm not blind!' His blue eyes showed disbelief.

'For heaven's sake!' She flew at him. 'It's not the easiest thing in the world to try to commiserate with someone when they've just lost their baby. Of course I'm upset!'

His face changed and became withdrawn. 'I didn't mean for you to take it all so personally.'

Melanie's heartbeat reflected her unease. 'Nurses spend a good part of their day counselling in one form or another,' she said dismissively, and hoped he would leave the whole subject alone. But it seemed he wasn't about to.

'So, what was your impression? Will Kiyo cope?'

'Yes...' Melanie took a deep breath and firmed her

voice. 'I'm sure she will. And at least she'll have the support of her husband. It's not nearly as soul-destroying as being on your own like—'

'Like you were?' Nick's question was so quiet it left a vacuum that was almost painful.

Dumbfounded, sick with disbelief, Melanie turned to him with excruciating slowness. 'How did you know?'

In an abrupt movement he changed speed, slamming the car into second gear and easing it off the strip of country road. He cut the engine and turned to her. 'A very belated gut feeling, Melanie. That's how I knew. You were obviously reluctant to get involved but I practically gave you no choice. I pushed you.' Self-disgust edged his voice into a low growl.

Melanie sat perfectly still and stared blindly ahead, her lips clamped together, barely under control.

Nick felt her pain and wished with all that was in him that he could help her. But she'd never let him. He knew that. And who could blame her? He'd already trampled all over her with his size nines! And yet...

'Melanie...'

She caught lingering traces of his aftershave as he leaned closer.

'Look—nothing heavy—but do you want to talk?'

Melanie averted her gaze and leaned back on the headrest, drawing in a long, shaky breath. 'No, Nick— I don't.'

'OK...' His voice was low and husky and he slowly withdrew.

Melanie heard him rev the motor and blanked her mind, only stirring when they'd crossed the railway line and entered the town proper. 'Could you let me off in the main street, please? I have to get groceries.'

'Why don't we have a coffee first?'

'No. Well, you don't have to... I'm all right...'

'You're not all right, Melanie.' He flicked up an eyebrow. 'Would you like me to run you straight home?'

'No, thanks.' She felt bewildered, cross with herself, cross with him. 'Let's have coffee.'

Nick growled a half-laugh. 'Anything to get me off your case, hmm?'

Melanie shook her head as if to clear it. Talking to Kiyo, she'd felt memories as sharp as glass rise up before her. She'd told Kiyo to think of the future now. She bit her lips together, twisting the strap of her shoulder-bag. Perhaps it was time she took her own advice.

She just wanted a quiet life. She swallowed a rueful snort. She'd be likely to get that with Nick Cavallo around! Why on earth did he make her feel threatened? So self-aware? And those deeply blue eyes positively unnerved her with their intuitive intelligence...

He parked neatly, just managing to squeeze between a farmer's utility and a battered campervan, its paintwork almost obliterated by faded holiday stickers.

As Nick cut the engine a keen-eyed small cattle dog, untethered in the back of the ute, trotted to the tailgate to peer at them through the windscreen, his uniquely pointed ears raised enquiringly.

'This must be a bit of a change for you.' Melanie's eyes met his briefly and slid away.

'Murrajong?' Nick released his seat belt and stretched his arms in a slow, relaxing arc. 'Mmm. Bit of a difference in the people too. They're very stoic. You're not a local?' He shot her a questioning blue glance.

'No. Sydney originally. I've been here about eighteen months.'

'Why Murrajong?'

Melanie lowered her gaze. 'I came here with my friend, Tamsin O'Shea,' she said, choosing her words carefully. 'We trained together in Sydney, then shared a flat for a while. When Tam's mother became ill she offered to come home. It was about then that I...wanted a change so Tam suggested I come too. Fortunately, there were jobs here for both of us. We share a house in the old part of town.'

'Tam O'Shea...' Nick narrowed his eyes thoughtfully. 'Would I have met her today in Theatre by any chance? Cute dimples? Amazing dark eyes?'

Melanie's smile was tinged with wryness. 'That's Tam. She works in Theatre.' She paused and then said almost as an afterthought, 'She's been the greatest friend.'

'You're lucky.' His voice was curiously flat and Melanie, suddenly ill at ease and not knowing why, reached for the doorhandle. 'Shall we get this coffee, then?'

* * *

'You've been here before,' she guessed, after the pleasant, middle-aged owner of the coffee-shop greeted Nick by name and showed them to a snugly private booth.

'A few times for breakfast,' he admitted, shifting round so that he could face her.

A fleeting frown touched her forehead. 'You're not living in the hospital quarters, then?'

'I lasted about forty-eight hours,' he confessed ruefully.

'They're pretty basic, I know. I don't know how Sean sticks it.' Melanie picked up the menu as if to study it.

'Do you have something going with Sean?' The question was delivered quietly and with care and she glanced up, surprised to see him deadly serious.

She gurgled a soft laugh. 'Of course I don't.'

'You seem—close. I can't think of another word.' He shrugged, as if mildly embarrassed.

Melanie cupped her chin and studied her companion for a moment. 'And we're only having coffee,' she pointed out half-mockingly.

'I know.' He looked down at the tablecloth and ran one long finger along its smooth surface. 'I'm just very careful where I tread these days, that's all,' he said shortly, and although his eyes were shuttered a tiny pulse beat at the corner of his mouth betrayed some unresolved emotion.

Melanie dropped her gaze, weighing and assessing. Had he been caught unintentionally in the cross-fire from a three-cornered love affair? She didn't know him well enough to ask and changed tack quickly. 'Sean's rather keen on Tam, actually.'

He laughed softly. 'You're not doing a spot of matchmaking on the side, are you?'

Melanie gave a slight lift to her shoulders and a determined smile. 'Personally, I think they'd be well suited. They're both very up-front kind of people. What you see is what you get.'

'Bully for them. Sounds very secure.' His mouth twisted with faint mockery and Melanie felt vaguely put down.

Nick Cavallo was obviously carrying some private pain, fighting bitter-sweet memories. She bit her lip, surprised that the idea gave her a peculiar pang.

'Let's have cinnamon toast to go with the coffee,' he suggested a little too heartily. 'Lunch seems a long time ago.'

'Fine.' Melanie gave him a speculative look.

'Sorry for my lapse back there.' His gruff apology sent her eyebrows up questioningly. 'I didn't mean to get heavy.' His mouth twisted with irony. 'It's been a weird kind of day, hasn't it?' He raked his fingers roughly through his hair. 'God! Let's not start talking shop.' The emotional charge his short outburst had created was, mercifully, diffused by the arrival of the waitress.

'Cappuccino?' Nick asked, and Melanie nodded. 'And cinnamon toast. Make mine a double order, please.' He looked a bit sheepish and Melanie couldn't help a chuckle. 'Have you found somewhere comfortable to live?'

His mouth tipped at the side. 'I'm leasing the Gilchrist place.'

'Crafters? The stone cottage on the highway?'

'That's the one.'

'I thought it was in disrepair.' Melanie showed surprise.

'Not any more. They've had it refurbished, especially for rental purposes. It came on the market only an hour or so before I enquired at the estate agent's.'

Melanie's eyes took on a dreamy look. 'I'd love to see what they've done with it.'

'Come out anytime,' Nick said expansively.

'I wouldn't be intruding?'

'No.' His face went blank. 'You wouldn't be intruding.'

'It's real Cotswold stone, you know,' she said conversationally. 'Originally shipped from England.'

'Is it? I dare say you're right.' He shrugged offhandedly. 'I know it's a damned sight more comfortable than the hospital accommodation.'

It was amazing what a hot drink and some food could do for your well-being. Melanie marvelled, savouring the last of the nutmegged froth from her coffee. Nick had set himself out to be relaxed and pleasant and she'd reciprocated and somehow it had worked. Perhaps they could be friends after all. Perhaps...

'That was wonderful, Nick. Thank you.' She fought back a feeling of shyness and placed her cup back on its saucer.

'At least you've got some colour back,' he said approvingly.

Melanie scrabbled for her bag.

She hovered uncertainly as he paid the bill and they walked outside together.

Nick rammed his hands into his trousers pockets, almost as if to avoid touching her. His blue eyes swept over her. 'I'll wait while you get your groceries,' he said brusquely. 'Give you a lift home.'

Melanie's heart reacted like a trapped bird. He was crowding her. Tucking a wayward frond of fair hair behind her ear, she quelled a sudden urge to run as far and as fast as she could. 'You don't have to wait Nick. I'll grab a taxi.'

He gave her one of his cryptic smiles. 'I don't mind.'

'But you've been on the go since two a.m.,' she protested weakly. 'Don't you want to get home?'

She could have sworn a shutter suddenly closed behind his eyes.

'I have nothing to get home for.'

Or did he mean no one? She struggled with several pertinent questions and then thought better of them.

'You're at it again, Melanie.'

She blinked. 'At what?'

'Sifting. Look, I've merely offered you a lift home. It's no big deal. If it'll make you feel better, I'll buy a paper and read it while I wait for you.' His mouth twitched. 'I haven't seen today's headlines yet. God only knows what riveting stuff I've missed.'

She'd been manipulated, as easily as that!

Melanie clamped her teeth on her lower lip and

began to cruise the aisles of the supermarket. Why on earth hadn't she written a shopping list?

Automatically, she threw bread, cereal and pasta into the trolley. Were they out of coffee? She took a jar just in case. At least she knew what they needed at the dairy case.

She selected fruit and vegetables at random and then saw what she'd done. What on earth was wrong with her? They never ate turnips...

I feel like I'm being ambushed, she thought grimly. *And* he read minds! She took a ragged breath, picturing Nick outside in his car waiting for her. It was the last thing she'd expected—or wanted.

Standing at the meat cabinet, she felt a wild feeling of panic clutch at her insides. The packaged cuts swam before her eyes and merged into one huge lump. She threw in what she thought they'd use and then paused with her hand on the edge of the refrigerated case. Should she ask Nick to stay for a meal?

Conflicting outcomes juxtaposed in her head and, still confused, she bent and hastily selected another steak.

She was all thumbs as she paid for her groceries at the check-out and then made her way outside and back up the street to Nick's car.

She peered in through the passenger window, seeing his dark head buried in the newspaper. She tapped gently and he looked up, slamming the newspaper shut and swinging out of the car.

It took only a few seconds to load the bags of groceries into the boot. 'You were quick.' He closed the boot and shot the trolley towards a nearby receiving bay.

Melanie gave a tinny laugh. 'It was a bit of a scatter-gun effort today, I'm afraid. I didn't have a list.' She looked around her and noticed that it was almost dark.

'You'll have to direct me, Melanie. I don't know where you live,' Nick said quietly, when they'd settled back into the car.

In the dim light she regarded him for a moment—the rather hawk-like profile, the well-shaped fingers on the steering-wheel, the whole of him. Vaguely, she noticed he'd swapped his jacket for a creamy-coloured bulky jumper. It looked very soft and warm. She resisted a silly urge to reach out and touch him...

'Hey...anyone home?'

'Oh, sorry.' She hauled in a steadying breath. 'Just keep on until the shops peter out. Then it's left into Cherry and right into Fisher's Lane.'

'Who was Fisher?'

She gave a smothered laugh. 'I have no idea, but Tam's grandmother probably would. She's in her seventies. Lived here all her life.'

'It must be something to have those kinds of roots...' His words trailed away.

In the dark of the car Melanie shrugged away suddenly bleak thoughts. It seemed neither of them had any such roots so it was pointless even surmising.

The gaunt old two-storied house was in darkness. For a brief moment Melanie had nurtured a hope that Tam would have made it home before her.

Nick leant across her and peered out. 'It looks huge. Do you have all of it?'

She shook her head, conscious of his warmth, his nearness, his maleness... She moved restlessly, reaching for the doorhandle.

'It's divided into two dwellings, euphemistically called townhouses.'

'So you have an upstairs and a downstairs.' He released her seat belt slowly, carefully. 'Nice neighbours?'

Melanie swallowed thickly. 'Jill and Roger Chandler. We hardly see them. They run the local pottery.'

Melanie juggled with the keys at the front door, every nerve end conscious of the man behind her. She finally got the right one in the lock and swung the door open, flooding the porch with soft light.

Her hand flicked uselessly at the light switch in the hall. 'Bulb must have blown,' she murmured, her throat dry.

Nick craned his neck towards the high ceiling. 'Have you a spare one? I'll put it in. How on earth do you get up there?'

'We've a ladder in the garage. Nick, watch where you're going.' She went forward cautiously in the gloom. 'Hang on, I'll get the light in the lounge.'

'Ah—that's better.' He looked interestedly about him at the bright cushions, the wall hangings, the books piled high on the floor. He cranked a dark eyebrow. 'Who's the reader?'

Melanie dipped her head and shrugged out of her

blazer. 'I am, actually. The kitchen's through here,' she said, leading the way.

Nick dropped the packages on the worktop and looked questioningly at her. 'Do you have that light bulb?'

'Oh, I'll just look...' Her heart was racing. She opened a top cupboard and scanned the contents. 'No... I had a feeling we'd used the last one. I'll get one tomorrow.'

He grinned fleetingly. 'Who'll climb on whose shoulders to put it in? You and Tam would hardly make the distance between you.'

They were almost touching. Their faces were mere centimetres apart and the sudden flare in his eyes set her senses whirling. 'I told you.' She steadied her breathing with difficulty. 'We have a ladder.' She looked away. 'Thanks for doing all this, Nick.'

'You're more than welcome.' He hunched forward, propping his hands on his lean hips. 'I guess I'd better make a move.'

'We'll be making a meal later, if you'd like to stay. There's plenty—'

'Some other time, perhaps. But thanks.'

She nodded and bit her lip. 'I'll walk out with you, then. Can't have you crashing into things.' She gave a choked laugh that sounded like a hiccup.

In the darkened hall he looked down at her. It seemed suddenly very quiet. 'Will you be all right?'

'Of course.' Don't go, she wanted to tell him. 'Tam should be home soon, anyway.'

'Until tomorrow, then,' he said with a somewhat strained smile.

They moved simultaneously towards the big central doorknob and collided awkwardly in the semi-darkness, bumping their heads.

'Oh! Sorry!'

'Are you OK?' Nick ran his fingers expertly over her temple.

'Yes, I think so.' Melanie looked bemusedly at him in the half-light. 'Are you?'

They were hanging on to one another, peering into each other's faces. Tiny tendrils of hair had come down and framed Melanie's almost oval-shaped face.

'Not really...' Nick's voice was huskily uneven. 'But I will be when I've done this...'

Melanie's breath fluttered out in a long sigh. His eyes seemed to hypnotise her until his lids lowered and he looked at her mouth and then his head came down and she went on tiptoe to meet him.

Her arms went round him and hugged him to her, her fingers closing instinctively on the soft stuff of his jumper as her body responded to the sweet shock of his kiss.

He took his time, savouring the taste of her mouth, exploring the softness of it, feeling for its shape and then experimenting with his tongue, until she opened her lips and allowed him to find his way inside.

One of his arms held her to him while the other, with fingers spread, stroked downwards to her hip and then up again, finding each of her ribs on the way, until it settled on the soft underswell of her breast.

Melanie made a tiny sound in her throat, sighing into his mouth. Oh, yes, she thought, her knees almost buckling. A flood of emotion swept through her, making her raise her arms and hold him loosely, then tighter. Sweet pain lanced downwards, twisted her insides. It had been so long...

It was much too soon when Nick broke from her and turned his head a little, smudging kisses across her cheek, her eyelids and into the soft curve of her throat, sending erotic visions to her mind and warmth along each vein.

Melanie clung to him, clung and clung, her cheek hard against the warmth of his chest, while his hands cradled her to him as though she were infinitely precious.

She had no clear idea whether they stood there for mere seconds or much longer. Finally, Nick's chest rose in a long sigh.

'Melanie... I should go.'

She drew back slowly, lifting weighted lids to stare bemusedly into his eyes. Yes, she supposed he should go. For lots of reasons none of this should have happened. And yet...there'd seemed a slow inevitability about it all.

He touched his thumb to her full lower lip. 'You OK?'

'I—think so,' she lied. It wasn't the time for postmortems. What they'd done they'd done. And it probably hadn't been very wise...

Watching her closely, Nick put her gently from him and then drew her back as if he couldn't help himself.

A strobe of light pierced the glass panel of the front door and they both turned towards it.

'Tam?' he said into her hair.

'Must be.'

The light disappeared down the driveway towards the garage.

Nick bent and kissed her one last time. Hard. She watched as he opened the door, fluttering a wave after him. But he didn't look back.

CHAPTER FOUR

'MEL? You in there?'

Melanie stepped back and closed the door, leaning against it for a moment while she mentally gathered her strength about her. Then, with her thoughts a mass of seething contradictions, she made her way along the darkened hall into the lounge.

'Hi. Sorry I left you with everything.' Tam tossed her shoulder-bag across to the settee. 'Gran was in high form,' she said wryly, plonking herself in an armchair and letting her long sweep of dark hair trail over the back. 'Sent her love, by the way. Were you seeing Nick out?'

Melanie hesitated, her heart doing wild jumps in her chest. Tam's bright, inquisitive eyes were missing nothing.

'It *was* his car I saw outside, wasn't it?'

Melanie sank weakly on to the nearest chair.

'Yes. He— We left the hospital about the same time. He gave me a lift.'

'Nice one.' Tam kicked off her shoes and curled neatly into the soft leather chair. 'I scrubbed for him today. Did he tell you? He's good. And I'm talking seriously skilled here.' She fixed Melanie with a faintly puzzled look. 'What's he doing, relieving in Murrajong?'

Melanie quickly swallowed the ache in her throat.

How could she be concerned about the nebulous reasons for his presence in the town when the reality was only too apparent?

Like the smell of him on her clothes. The taste of him on her mouth. And, because of some very basic chemistry between them, she, like a fool, had lowered her fragile defences and let him in...

'He didn't say, Tam. And I didn't feel like probing.' Agitatedly, she hugged her arms around her midriff as a kind of buffer.

Tam's dark head tipped sideways, her almost black eyes full of speculation. 'Do you have something to tell me, Melanie?'

'No.' Melanie let her head go back onto the soft leather. 'And don't start a fishing expedition, Tam,' she warned. 'Sean was asking after you again,' she side-tracked smoothly. 'I'm starting to feel like his agony aunt.'

Tam went still. 'Sean Casey?'

Melanie rolled her eyes. 'Is there another Sean in A and E?'

'What did he say?' Her eyes cast down, Tam pleated the denim across her shapely thigh.

'Nothing much. Waffled on a bit.'

'Mel-an-ie...' Tam warned, picking up a small, soft cushion threateningly.

'OK, OK.' A brief smile curved Melanie's mouth. 'I think he's gearing up to ask you out.'

Tam looked blank.

'Well?' Melanie frowned. 'Will you go if he asks you?'

'I might,' Tam proclaimed airily.

'You're kidding me! I thought you liked him!'

'I do.' Tam's smile was cat-like mysterious. 'Sean's a real spunk.'

Nick hardly knew how he'd got home.

The utter sweetness of Melanie's sensuality had hit him like an avalanche. But where did he go from here? Nowhere, if he had any sense at all! His mouth straightened into a hard line. He'd only kissed her, for crying out loud. But if her friend hadn't come home when she had...

Hell! Turned on, like a randy adolescent! He swore explicitly, his fingers rattling over the glasses in the cabinet. He took the shot of neat whisky, threw it back and poured another, looking at it for a moment. Getting mildly drunk wasn't the solution, he thought in disgust, capping the bottle and returning it to the cupboard.

There was no sign of Nick, thank goodness. Melanie reclaimed some of her equilibrium with a sharply indrawn breath. The early shift was under way and her stomach felt tied in knots.

Where did they go from here? Now they'd crossed the line, so to speak, would he want more from her? Perhaps he'd put the whole episode out of his mind already. Put it down to emotional overload, after the rather brutal day they'd had. She couldn't second-guess him.

Her own reactions were still fluid. What she'd done—kissing him like that—had seemed like an erotic dream this morning. After Aaron her emotions had been bludgeoned into an almost inoperable state. But just yesterday they'd come screamingly alive, pushing to the surface through every pore of her skin... Her heart hitched to a halt. For heaven's sake! There was work to be done.

By the look of it, their first walking wounded for the day had arrived, a burly farmer, hanging rather grimly to the arm of his slender little wife. Putting on a professional face, Melanie went forward to greet them.

'Mr and Mrs Griffen, isn't it?' She remembered the couple from a fundraiser for the hospital.

'Colin and Maureen,' the woman nodded. 'Col's hurt his foot.'

'Damn great cow stood on me.' He grimaced as Melanie helped him straight inside to the examination couch.

She frowned over the rapidly swelling foot.

'Weren't you wearing shoes, Mr Griffen?'

'He was wearing tatty old sneakers,' his wife interposed, 'even though I'd bought him a proper pair of work boots for the dairy.'

'They're tight on me feet, Maureen. I told you that...' The big man looked mournful and Melanie hid a smile.

'I'll get one of the doctors to look at you. You'll probably have to trot along for an X-ray.'

'How long's all this gonna take, lovey? I got a farm to run.'

'Col, belt up,' Maureen Griffen said bluntly. 'It's not Sister's fault and it's certainly not mine so, for once in your life, just do what you're told.'

Colin Griffen opened his mouth, shut it again and grinned sheepishly at Melanie. 'Young Dr Casey about?'

'I'll just see,' she offered, working hard on keeping her face straight as she detailed Fiona to find the resident.

Seconds later Sean sauntered in, his white coat pushed back on his hips. 'G'day, Col.' He grinned, seeming mightily amused at the big man's plight. 'Been kicking doors in, have you?'

'Yeah—right. What do you reckon, Doc? Is it broken?'

'That's what the X-ray will tell us, Col.'

Col swore colourfully under his breath.

'The kids will just have to muck in,' Sean said, and winked slyly at Melanie. She left them to it.

A trickle of emergencies kept her busy for the next little while. At least Tammy Wells, one of their enrolled nurses, was back on duty and that was helping to spread the workload a little more evenly. Melanie looked at her watch, deciding she could safely squirrel away a few minutes for her paperwork.

'I'll be in my office,' she told Tammy with a calmness she was far from feeling, and made her way swiftly towards the sunny small room adjoining Reception.

'Got a minute, Melanie?'

She whipped around, the sight of Nick sending her heart into overdrive. Quickly averting her eyes, she managed a suitably detached smile. 'Come on in.'

When they were both seated she looked up expectantly, and for the first time noticed he was carrying a sheaf of papers. So it was business. She felt diminished, a bit let down, because she'd thought—

'I've managed to secure the services of a locum.'

Her shoulder twitched. 'That was quick.'

Nick's eyes seemed to track over her features one by one, then flicked back to the papers in front of him on the desk. 'I've used this particular agency in Brisbane once or twice. They've always come up trumps.'

'So, who've they got for us?' Melanie feigned lightness, scraping together her ragged defences.

'Ah...' Nick bent his head and checked the faxed information. 'Dr Glen Fielding. Arriving on this evening's plane.'

'Is someone meeting him?'

'Her.'

'Sorry?'

He curved her a brief smile. 'It's Dr *Glenda* Fielding.'

'Oh.' Melanie quashed an inexplicable ruffle of pique. 'So, is she out of work or what?'

Nick tugged thoughtfully at his bottom lip. 'Contracted to take up a position with a Brisbane suburban practice, apparently. Not due to start for another month and happy to give us a couple of weeks in the meantime.'

He picked up one of Melanie's pens, tapping it end to end. 'I offered to meet her but she was quite firm about finding her own way here. Obviously, an independent lady.'

Somewhere in the back of her mind Melanie heard him speaking, but her eyes were on his mouth and her mind on the way he'd kissed her last night. Had it meant anything at all to him? And if it had would he tell her? Talk to her? Oh, Lord, this was awful. Her stomach began to churn.

'Do some of the taxi fleet meet the plane?' Nick shot her a sharp look. 'I'd hate our locum to be stranded.'

Melanie swallowed. 'There'll be someone there,' she affirmed quietly, 'but you'd better let the accommodation officer know what's happening.'

'All done.' He tossed the pen aside and got to his feet. 'I'll be around if you need me, OK?'

Her heart pounding, she waited until he was almost at the door. 'Nick—'

He turned and waited.

She clenched her hands so hard her knuckles turned white. 'I— It's nothing important,' she mumbled, her courage wafting away like smoke from an extinguished flame.

She looked down at her paperwork in bleak despair as he departed. It was obvious he didn't give a damn about her. He'd probably rationalised kissing her as getting rid of his frustrations, she thought darkly, hating her doubts yet grabbing at them in sick uncertainty.

It was almost a relief of a kind, a return to normality, when the emergency phone rang outside. As Melanie scribbled details Fiona and Tammy hovered to get a sniff of what was coming in. 'Where's Dr Cavallo?' she demanded, slamming down the phone.

'Here.' Nick had come up light-footedly behind her.

Shoving her personal pain aside, she turned to him. 'Explosion in the science room at the high school. Two boys. Thirteen-year-olds. Burns.'

'Ambulance there?'

Melanie grimaced. 'Both out on other calls.'

'Both? I thought we had three?'

'One's under repair.'

Nick swore softly. 'In that case, we'd better get over there. Dr Casey!' he bellowed, and Sean came, running. 'Melanie and I have an emergency at the high school. You're in charge. Don't take any flak from anyone.'

The registrar directed a sharp glance at Melanie. 'You up for this?'

Her heart did an odd tattoo. 'Of course.'

'Let's gather up what we'll need, then. Better prepare for the worst scenario,' he added grimly, as they sped down the corridor, and Melanie knew he meant the possibility of full thickness burns where the whole of the underlying tissues would be critically at risk.

Her soft, vulnerable mouth tightened. Poor kids! Whatever way you looked at it, their injuries almost certainly meant pain.

With quick precision she organised the emergency drug box, dressing packs and IV cut-down tray, praying fervently they wouldn't need it. With burns, however, anything was possible, and if the skin on the kids' bodies had been badly damaged it would make it nigh impossible to access a vein in the usual way. Nick would have to execute a surgical procedure to get an IV in.

Melanie secured the pack. She just hoped his surgical skills were up to scratch. Tam seemed to think they were…

'Can we help, Sister?'

Melanie spun back, almost tripping over Fiona and Tammy who had been following like puppies. 'Yes, you can,' she said crisply. 'Tammy, grab a couple of space blankets, please. Fiona, ring Mr Lamb at the high school and tell him we're on our way. Now!'

Despite the reasons for it, Melanie felt a dizzying feeling of *déjà vu*, sitting beside Nick in the Jaguar.

'What's the situation with the ambulance?' he barked, shooting out of the parking bay and accelerating towards the main gates.

Her stomach lurched and then settled. 'One ambulance has gone to an outlying farm to collect a midwifery patient in premature labour. The other is at the strip, waiting for the air ambulance to arrive from Brisbane.'

'Ferrying patients home?'

'Yes.' Melanie looked at him quickly. Something was still hanging in the air between them. Something elemental. As undefined as it was unfinished…

'The base said they'll redirect that ambulance to the high school and ask the air crew to hang on until we see what condition the kids are in.'

Nick grunted. 'Anything like serious, they'll need the burns unit at the Royal. We have no facilities to treat them indefinitely. As it is, we should have an extra pair of hands with us on this jaunt.'

Biting her lips together, Melanie could only silently agree.

Alan Lamb, the school principal, seemed over-whelmingly relieved to see them.

'Good of you to come so quickly,' he said, as Nick made quick introductions. 'Sister Stewart.' He looked faintly distracted. 'We've met, of course. The rubella talk for the year eights, wasn't it? It's a bad business,' he continued, visibly upset by what had happened in his school. 'Very bad.'

'We've put the lads into sick bay for the moment.' He led them swiftly along the wide, partly enclosed verandah that held rows of student lockers and sports paraphernalia.

'Was there a teacher present when the accident happened?' Nick asked abruptly.

'Phoebe Lyons,' the principal confirmed. 'She's very young. Murrajong's her first appointment. But she's coped magnificently.' Mr Lamb's voice roughened slightly. 'Administered first aid and calmed the class like a teacher with twenty years' experience.'

'Nevertheless, you'll need to keep an eye on her,' Nick warned. 'Post-traumatic shock can be a serious matter.'

'Understood, Doctor.' Agitatedly, the principal brushed a hand through his greying hair. 'None of it was her fault, in any case. The boys took it upon themselves to add a double dose of hardener to what was a very straightforward formula for epoxy resin.'

Melanie stifled a gasp of horror. She knew enough about chemicals to realise that spontaneous combustion would have occurred, and resulting burns to the boys terrifyingly inevitable. She turned her head.

Nick's face was like granite as they turned into the room being used as a sick bay.

'Thank God, you've come!'

Phoebe Lyons looked as though she was holding herself together by a thread. 'I hope I've done the right thing.' Her small dark head swung back restlessly, almost as if she were afraid to take her eyes off her pupils for a second.

Nick and Melanie exchanged glances. One boy was sitting hunched over at a sink, his injured hand dangling under a stream of water. 'That's fine,' Nick reassured the young teacher briefly. 'What about the other lad?'

Phoebe bit her lip. 'Not so good, I'm afraid. The flame caught him as he bent over the Bunsen burner—ran up the side of his throat and into his hair. He's lying down—' Her composure crumpled.

'You've done all you possibly could, Phoebe,' Nick said gently. 'We'll take over now. Mr Lamb!' he barked. 'If you wouldn't mind...'

'Oh, yes of course.' The principal moved quickly to usher the distressed young woman outside.

'This might be a bit rough, Melanie.'

'I won't faint on you,' she said thinly, tossing Nick a sterile pack of gloves and snapping open her own.

With one accord they moved to the boy who was lying frighteningly still, his face towards the wall.

Melanie had steeled herself for the horrendous task of having to cut away the youngster's clothing, but one glance told her it was too late for that.

The burn had taken all before it right up into the

boy's scalp, and it was going to take a skilled surgeon, using special solvents and fine scalpels, to remove the minute particles of clothing still adhering
to the child's burned skin.

Melanie realised she was holding her breath and
let it go. It was taking all her self-control not to flinch
from the shiny, marble-like mass which only minutes
ago had been healthy, youthful skin.

It took Nick barely seconds to make his assess-
ment as he flicked his stethoscope across the boy's
chest, his face registering his grim findings.

'The kid's borderline,' he snapped. 'Five hundred
normal saline, stat.'

Her face tight, Melanie was already swabbing the
site to get a line in.

The boy whimpered and groaned.

'You're OK, son.' Nick hunkered down beside
him and uttered words of reassurance, his tone calming, gentle.

Melanie pressed her lips together as she watched
him, doubting whether the child was registering anything at all.

Nick glanced up at her. His mouth was white-
ringed, tight with tension. 'Let's give the poor little
blighter some pain relief. I'd say he's about forty-
five to fifty kilos, but we'll err on the side of caution.
Make it twenty-five milligrams of pethidine IV and
ten of Maxolon.'

Melanie began willing her own strength into the
boy as she prepared the drugs.

'We'll keep monitoring him,' Nick said quietly. 'If
the ambulance isn't here pronto, we'll consider an-

other ten to fifteen milligrams in twenty minutes or so.'

'Burns are such cruel injuries,' Melanie breathed. Her heart was fearful. The boy had been so close to crashing but, miraculously, they'd got to him in time. But that had been only the first step. Medical skill was needed now to pull him back. Would it be enough, though? she wondered. Or would the day end in tragedy…?

'OK?' Nick murmured close to her ear.

She swallowed. Her face felt tight, aching. 'I'll just get a sterile dressing on…'

Nick touched her shoulder. 'As soon as you're ready, we'll check the other lad.'

At a glance, Melanie could see that the second boy's skin damage was barely of partial thickness magnitude. Burn blisters were already forming, which augured well. The skin was an amazing healer of itself, and with scrupulous hygiene the hand should be well on the way to recovery in a couple of weeks.

She looked across to judge Nick's reaction, seeing his jaw tighten, before he said brusquely, 'You've been lucky. Bloody stupid thing to do, though, wasn't it?'

The youngster nodded, two large tears tracking unchecked down his cheeks.

Melanie bit her lip, wondering at Nick's seemingly hard approach, but held her tongue. The boy was beginning to shiver.

'What's your name, son?' Nick began unwrapping the space blanket.

'R-Rhys Evans, sir.'

Nick's eyebrows lifted fractionally. 'And your mate?'

The boy sniffed, dragging in a huge, uneven breath. 'Chris Treloar.'

'Mike's son?' Melanie looked at Nick in horror.

'Problem?'

'Could be.'

Nick inclined his head, silently taking on board all the possible implications of the situation. He rested his hand briefly on the boy's fair head. 'Take it easy now, sunshine. Sister Stewart will give you something for the pain. We'll need you in hospital for a short while, but you'll be fine. Back playing footy next season, no worries.'

'Have they let your parents know, Rhys?' Melanie asked gently, as she prepared the boy's arm to receive the saline drip and painkiller.

'Yeah...' The youngster scraped the back of his uninjured hand across his eyes. 'Mum's coming.'

'Right, Sister,' Nick said tersely. 'Let's see what's keeping that ambulance, shall we? Where the hell is Mike?' he growled, when they were out of earshot.

Melanie drew in a jagged breath. 'It's very serious with Chris, isn't it?'

Nick was grim-faced. 'Yes, it's serious. Tissue death is imminent. We need him under an anaesthetic, like now!'

Melanie swallowed thickly. It was imperative for the destroyed tissues to be removed. Left unattended, they could be the starting point of a bacterial infection and God knew what else...

Nick tugged at his tie, as if it were choking him. 'What's Mike's marital situation?'

'Separated,' Melanie said tautly. 'They split up last year. Liz left town. Wanted to take Chris with her but he opted to stay with his father.'

'Messy.' Nick shook his head. 'Hell's bells, where is he? We're going to need a signature to operate.'

Melanie touched his arm. 'There's Mike now.'

Nick spun to peer out through the large picture window. Mike Treloar, in tracksuit and trainers, was running at speed across the quadrangle.

'Keep an eye on our patients, Melanie,' Nick instructed, his hand resting briefly on her shoulder. 'I'll intercept Mike. Try to break it to him gently.'

With a hard, indrawn breath and a flurry of very mixed emotions, she watched him dash outside and take the steps two at a time. Then everything began to happen at once.

Two teams of ambulance officers arrived with stretchers. Following them along the verandah was Mr Lamb, accompanied by a distraught-looking Mrs Evans. In jeans and oversized checked shirt, the mother looked as though she'd dropped whatever farm work she'd been doing and had come, running, to her child's side.

Melanie swallowed the lump in her throat, reaching out unobtrusively to pluck a long piece of straw from the woman's hair. 'Rhys has been wonderfully brave,' she said, and drew Marnie Evans across to her son.

As she repacked their medical kit Melanie realised she felt out of kilter, her nerves stretched to shreds.

Having children was such an awesome responsibility...

'Are you all right?' Nick was beside her, looking less grim but still tense.

'Fine,' she lied glibly. 'How's Mike?'

'Not good.' Nick grimaced. 'Worried sick about his wife's reaction. Said she'll have his guts for garters for this lot. Go for legal custody of Chris.'

Melanie tutted softly. 'How could it be Mike's fault?' She swung round, experiencing a sudden pang of alarm. Mike Treloar looked terrible, his arms knotted around his body as if he were in pain. 'I'll speak to him,' she said quietly.

'Did you get through to him?' Nick asked later as he secured the sharps they'd used for safe disposal at the hospital.

'Who knows? Are we ready to go, then?' She hitched up the bag expectantly.

'Ah...' Nick followed her gaze to where the ambulancemen were attempting to ease a stretcher through the narrow doorway. 'Would you be prepared to hang on here for a bit?'

'Sorry?' She stared at him confusedly, and Nick frowned slightly.

'Alan Lamb asked if one of us could speak briefly to the kids who were present when the explosion happened. In layman's terms, explain the boys' injuries, their probable treatment, how long they'll be away from school—that kind of thing. Apparently, they're still pretty shocked, and waiting for a school counsellor to fly out could take days. He doesn't want to send the kids home from school today in a kind of limbo about what's happened to their class-mates.'

'Fearful in their ignorance,' Melanie murmured, letting the bag slip down off her shoulder onto the floor. 'OK, I don't mind speaking to them.'

'You don't have to, you know,' Nick was quick to point out. 'It's certainly not part of your job description.'

'For heaven's sake!' Melanie was caught between irritation and impatience. 'There's no need to wait around until we all hang ourselves with red tape. I'll do it. All right?'

He ignored her sarcasm. 'You'd better clear it with your supervisor, then. Hadn't you?'

Melanie heard his brusque reminder and gritted her teeth. 'I imagine Mr Lamb would allow me to phone from his office. Are you going with the ambulance?'

'I am. Speaking of which, you'll need my car to get back.' Fishing in his pocket, he presented her with his keys. 'Just go easy with your foot,' he instructed, as if she were about to take her driver's test. 'She's a bit quick on the uptake.'

'Aren't you worried I'll run it up a gum tree?' Melanie questioned facetiously.

Dark humour spilled into his eyes and pulled at the corner of his mouth. 'I'm insured.'

CHAPTER FIVE

'WELL, how did it go?' Suzy asked when Melanie finally made an appearance at the nurses' station. 'Nick said you'd stayed on to debrief the kids after the accident.'

'Mmm.' Melanie gave a wry smile. 'It went OK, I think. They were upset to some extent about their classmates. Asked a thousand questions. Got a bit gruesome towards the end. Little horrors.'

'Sounds about right.' Suzy chuckled. 'Want some coffee? I've just made litres.'

'No, thanks, Suz. Mr Lamb put on morning tea, including home-made sponge.'

'Oh, way to go... I haven't had sponge cake for ages. What kind was it?'

'You twit.' Melanie laughed softly. 'It was ginger, actually. With whipped cream.' She let her gaze drift casually around. 'Is Nick about? I need to return his car keys.'

Suzy eyed her contemporary over the mountain of files she was sorting. 'Still in Theatre with Chris Treloar. Charlie asked for him, apparently.'

Melanie opened her mouth to comment then closed it abruptly. Charles Hunt was the hospital's general surgeon. If he'd decided Nick had expertise he could harness, he certainly would have had no qualms about seconding him.

'Nick looked pretty uptight.' Suzy rested her small chin in her upturned hand. 'I don't blame him. From what I saw, the kid's lucky to be alive.'

'Oh, Suzy, don't.' Melanie suppressed a shudder. 'They'll transfer him to Brisbane, of course.'

'As soon as he's stable. Late this afternoon, Nick thought.' Suzy looked suddenly thoughtful. 'I get the impression our relieving reg. has a lot more surgical skills than he's letting on.'

Melanie stayed very still. The same thought had also occurred to her. Yet she had nothing tangible to hang the premise on—just a feeling. She looked up. Suzy's head was bent over her work once more and Melanie breathed a sigh of relief. Nick Cavallo's status as a doctor was nothing she wanted to talk about—except maybe with him.

'Suz, if you need me for anything, I'll be in my office.'

'Right-o.' The RN's bright little face fell into an easy grin and Melanie made her exit thankfully.

It was much later in the day when Melanie was able to return Nick's keys to him. She caught up with him as he was heading back to his office.

'Thanks,' he said briefly, and held the door open for her, taking it for granted she wanted an audience. 'Have a seat,' he invited.

Melanie's heart fluttered a bit and she shook her head. 'I can't stay. I have hand-over shortly.'

'So.' Nick backed up against the desk with his arms folded. 'How did it go with the kids this morning?'

'Fine.' Melanie reached out and gripped the back of the chair. 'They asked some pretty intelligent questions, actually. I encouraged them to keep in touch with the boys, especially Chris as he'll be away the longest. They came up with the idea of compiling a class letter each week to keep him up to date.'

'That's good,' Nick said quietly. 'Excellent. His morale is all-important at this stage.'

'How is he, really?' Melanie asked and Nick made himself comfortable on the edge of the desk.

'Better than we could have hoped.' His face sobered and she saw the tension of concentration still lingering there. 'It'll be a long haul, of course, but his face is basically untouched and his hair will grow back—so, all in all, not a bad prognosis.'

'Oh, that's a relief!' Melanie felt some of her own anxiety drain away. 'And Mike? I haven't seen him…'

'In Recovery with Chris. He'll go in the air ambulance with him, of course. He's got a few days' leave owing to him, and after that I gather the grandparents will take over the visiting role and so on. Mike will get down to Brisbane when he can.'

'Has he contacted Liz?' Melanie queried.

'I didn't ask.'

'Surely he wouldn't do anything so foolish as not contacting her?'

Nick's eyebrows rose. 'We can't interfere, Melanie.'

'Who's talking about interfering?' Melanie responded quickly with a surge of anger. 'Whatever their marital problems, Liz is still the boy's mother. She has a right to know what's happened.'

To her surprise, Nick said slowly, 'Yes, she does.' He thought for a moment. 'OK. I see your point. I'll make it my business to speak with him. Come at him from a professional standpoint—whether seeing his mother will reassure Chris or vice versa. That should elicit some definitive response from him.'

Melanie bit her lip. 'I could speak to Mike just as well…'

'No, Melanie.' Nick was terse. 'Leave it to me.'

His eyes locked with hers, penetratingly blue, soaking up colour from the soft theatre pyjamas. 'Sorry.' His mouth turned down. 'I didn't mean to come on heavy.' With a sigh he half turned and dragged a hand wearily through his dark hair, strands of which fell back on his forehead, giving him a faintly dissolute air. 'Was there anything else we needed to discuss?'

Melanie was struggling to resist the musky lure of his maleness, shaken by the intensity of emotion which just standing next to him generated throughout her entire body.

What about last night? she wanted to ask him. Was it the same for you? Or was all it had implied over already? Had it been mistimed, stupid, hasty—emotional overload after a brutal day? Or just the beginning of something—

'Talk to me, Melanie.'

'Sorry…' Embarrassed, she shrank back into her own private space. 'There's nothing, really…'

An odd expression came into his eyes and his hand

reached out briefly to brush her cheek. 'See you tomorrow, then.'

She nodded and grabbed for the door, hauling it open, her slender form a twist of pale blue as she fled out into the corridor.

As far as her job was concerned, Melanie had never been a clock-watcher, but by Friday afternoon she was willing the end of her shift.

The weekend lay ahead—two days of relative peace and quiet, which she would use to try and sort out her feelings about Nick. With their paths continually crossing at work, she'd felt on an emotional sea-saw.

At least the arrival of their locum, Glenda Fielding, had provided a kind of buffer between herself and Nick, Melanie thought with an odd kind of relief. The female medico was proving more than capable. And friendly, settling into their team with hardly a ripple.

With a muted sigh, Melanie turned her attention back to the department's budget on which she was working. She'd found a quiet corner in the sun lounge and had almost got her figures to balance. They were running close to the wind, though. She frowned, nibbling the end of her pen. Perhaps it was time to think about another fundraiser...

'Why is no one attending to the child in the examination room?' The sharp question came from behind her.

Melanie jerked her head up and sideways to connect with Nick's accusing blue gaze. Her hackles rose, along with her defences. 'I thought Dr Fielding was.'

His dark brows drew together. 'Well, clearly, Sister, she's not.'

'She must have been called elsewhere, then.' Melanie swallowed hard, the now-familiar drift of his cologne teasing at her nostrils.

'Shall we, then?' It was more an order than a request and Melanie stood, shutting her ledger with a snap. She felt unfairly put-upon. With Suzy's presence the department was running at full strength again. There was no reason why he couldn't have found someone else to assist him.

'Do you have the details?' he asked shortly, as they made their way towards the examination cubicle.

Melanie dragged her thoughts together. 'Sally Cooper, aged eleven. Fell during warm-up exercises at her ballet class.' And it's not exactly life-threatening, she felt like adding, perceiving him to have already accused her of incompetence, albeit obliquely.

Sally turned out to have nothing more serious than a twisted ankle.

'It'll be uncomfortable for a few days,' Nick told Mrs Cooper, who was looking on anxiously, 'but Sally should mobilise it in moderation. Some appropriate physio should help as well.'

'She has exams in a month's time, Doctor.'

'It should be fine by then.' Nick directed a warm smile at the child and helped her up.

'You should both come to our end-of-year recital.'

Mrs Cooper sent a hopeful look at Nick and Melanie. 'It's a wonderful night and they always do some Christmassy thing at the end. And, of course, we're always happy to sell another couple of tickets,' she said with a laugh.

Nick's gaze trapped Melanie's and then became shuttered. 'It sounds like a night for the stars. Wouldn't you agree, Sister?'

'Absolutely.' Melanie drummed up a smile. Wretched man! Why didn't he just say he wouldn't be buying any tickets? He wouldn't even be around by the end of the year.

'Sorry for deserting you,' Glen apologised to Melanie later. 'I'll bet Nick was less than impressed.'

Melanie shrugged and said nothing. She already felt offside enough with the man. 'I should have double-checked, anyway,' she said. 'Got Sean.'

'No, you couldn't.' Glen tucked a stray frond of dark hair behind her ear. 'Nick sent him off early. Heavy date tonight, hasn't he?'

Melanie groaned. She'd almost forgotten. 'With my friend and flatmate, Tam O'Shea. It's been weeks in the making.'

'Oh, how gorgeous. And you're caught in the middle?'

'It feels a bit like that lately.' Melanie's hands moved to plug in the kettle. 'Coffee?'

'Mmm. I'd kill for one. Sean said they're going dancing.' Glen got mugs down from the shelf.

'So I believe.' Melanie's eyes were faintly wistful. 'They're both great movers. Tam's invited him to eat with us first, though. Heaven knows what she's planning.'

Glen laughed, showing even white teeth. 'I'll think of you when I'm enjoying my Chinese take-away.'

'You're on duty?'

'All weekend. I don't mind, though,' she added quickly. 'I'm here to work and Nick's well overdue for some time off.'

'Come on, Mel, get a move on,' Tam exhorted, as Melanie scrambled into the red Barina after work.

'Sorry. Hand-over took forever for some reason.'

'You're too accommodating to everyone, that's your trouble,' Tam grumbled, and they took off in a spurt of gravel.

'I thought I'd do a chicken dish tonight.' She turned to Melanie with a question in her eyes. 'Does Sean like chicken?'

'Put it between a burger bun and he'll eat anything.' Melanie snickered.

'I'm nervous, Mel. Isn't it weird?'

A glint of mischief lit Melanie's eyes. 'Take heart, then, ducky. I have a feeling Sean is, too. I saw him in and out of the men's a bit today.'

'Oh, poor baby!'

'Don't you dare say I told you,' Melanie warned.

'Would I?'

After a minute Melanie said, 'Tam, I've been thinking…'

'Mmm?'

'Well, are you sure I won't be in the way tonight?

I mean, I could easily go down to the squash centre and get a game—'

'Don't you dare!' Tam's agitation transferred itself to the accelerator, and the car surged forward along the bitumen.

Melanie clutched at her seat belt. 'That was one of Col Griffen's cows you nearly maimed,' she complained mildly.

Tam looked innocent. 'What was it doing on the road?'

'Good question.' Melanie rolled her eyes heavenward and hoped they'd get home in one piece.

Melanie had just finished wiping down the bench tops and putting the last plate away when the doorbell rang, startling her.

She glanced at the little carriage clock on top of the fridge. Nine o'clock. Jill or Roger, she decided with a wry smile. On the borrow, probably. They worked such long hours that they never seemed to have time to do a proper shop.

'Coming,' she called, making her way along the hallway. Opening the big, oak-panelled door, she lifted a hand to activate the porch light.

'Nick!' She scooped in a sharp breath.

'I'm whacked,' he said, and looked at her. Light flared briefly behind him, accentuating the deep grooves of weariness in his lean face. 'And I had to see you.'

CHAPTER SIX

MELANIE blinked in confusion and found herself drawing Nick inside to the warmth.

'Are you just getting home?' Her voice rose in disbelief. He should have been off duty ages ago.

'Thanks to two young fools who'd been drag-racing on mountain bikes. They collided at speed.'

'Ouch!' She made the comment to try to cover her scattered thoughts. 'I had to see you,' he'd said. That could mean anything... 'Much damage?'

Nick rubbed his forehead with a long finger. 'Busted ribs, fractured cheek-bone, dislocated shoulder, numerous cuts and abrasions.' He grimaced. 'I helped Glen sort them out, but it was like a madhouse, with both sets of parents bawling one another out and then bawling the kids out.'

Without thinking, she led him through to the kitchen. 'Let's hope it's a relatively quiet night from here on in, then.'

'Amen to that.'

'I'll get you something to eat. You must be starved...' Swallowing, Melanie floundered to a halt. They were both talking for the sake of it. He was beside her, so close, seeming to tower over her in the small kitchen.

'Melanie?' Those incredible blue eyes locked with hers in silent query.

Her heart stopped and seemed to tremble.

'I didn't come here for your food.'

'Oh…' She tipped her head back just as his arms reached out and hauled her in close, shaping her so completely to his body that she felt his hard flex of muscle. The sweet sting of anticipation robbed her of thought.

'I've been wanting to do this for days…' His mouth was buried against her hair. 'You've got to me, Melanie Stewart.' Very slowly, he pulled back to look at her.

Melanie stayed very still, afraid to move lest she broke the spell that held them captive. Suddenly Nick grimaced, and she detected a tautness about him as he let her go.

'You must think I'm an idiot, coming here like this…'

Her hands came up and cupped the back of his head, drawing his face down to hers. 'An exhausted idiot,' she qualified, her lips curving sweetly. 'Sit down and I'll get you a glass of wine.'

'Thanks. Oh, I'm driving,' he added a bit half-heartedly, dropping onto a chair at the head of the pine table.

With her back towards him, Melanie was able to suck in a few calming breaths. 'The food will soon soak it up,' she said, using all her control not to spill the dark red wine she placed in front of him.

'You're determined to feed me, then?' His eyes swept her face in a brief caress.

'It's lime and chili chicken.' She placed her hands beside him on the table, as if to reclaim her space somehow. 'I only need to heat it up in the micro-wave. And there's plenty,' she added, uncovering the large casserole dish. 'We fed Sean.'

'Ah.' Nick savoured his wine in a long swallow. 'Did they get off all right?'

Melanie's laugh tinkled. 'Finally. After Tam changed her outfit about four times. They should have a fun night, anyway.'

'Speaking of fun...' Nick stared down into his glass '...my barging in here hasn't upset your own plans for the evening, has it?' For the first time he appeared to notice her elegant black leggings and hand-woven red top.

'I have no plans, Nick,' she said quietly, scooping a generous portion of chicken into a microwave-proof dish. 'There's rice, too. Would you like some?' She paused with the spoon in the air.

He nodded. 'Sounds good. Thanks. I have the weekend off.'

Melanie looked up from setting the timer on the microwave. He looked as chuffed as a schoolboy granted an extra half-day.

'I suppose you're heading off to Brisbane.' She tried to sound casual, valiantly trying to ignore the way her heart lurched at the prospect.

One eyebrow flicked upwards. 'Why would I be going to Brisbane?'

Melanie shrugged. 'Girlfriend, perhaps?' The very thought sent butterflies zigzagging around her stomach in wild pursuit of each other.

'Apart from my mother, I have no personal ties in Brisbane these days,' he said flatly.

Relief, for which she had no clear explanation, flooded Melanie's whole being. 'What are you going to do with yourself, then?' She feigned lightness, setting the place before him with neat, graceful movements.

'I'm going skydiving.'

'Out of a plane?'

'Of course, out of a plane.' Nick looked amused, dangling his glass loosely between his fingers.

'But isn't that dangerous?' Wide eyes projected her unease as she imagined his body smashed to pieces after a jump gone wrong.

'Not if you're fit and know what you're doing,' he justified. 'I've done over a hundred jumps and the club here is very professional. I've had a couple of jumps with them already.'

'We had someone in recently with both ankles broken after a bungled parachute jump,' Melanie said darkly, busying herself with dishing up his meal and setting it before him.

'Probably a tangled chute or an unusually heavy landing,' Nick said casually. 'I'm flattered you're concerned about my welfare, though.' Picking up his fork, he sent her a very sexy smile which sent her heart into overdrive. 'This is good,' Nick said, setting about the meal with obvious relish.

'Tam made it.' Melanie set water to boil for coffee later and then, not knowing what to do, poured herself a small measure of wine and joined him at the table.

Her thoughts ran riot. So he didn't have a current girlfriend, but he certainly had a recent past. Of that she was sure. She'd seen shadows lurking in his eyes when he'd thought himself unobserved. Well, for heaven's sake, her rational self argued, the man is thirty-four. Of course he'd have had relationships, lovers—as she'd had. Well, one at least. One that had left her acutely vulnerable and with a residue of hurt a horse couldn't jump over...

'Don't be so hard on yourself, Melanie.' Nick chased the last morsel of chicken around his plate and ate it with relaxed enjoyment. 'And stop taking life so seriously,' he went on frankly, 'otherwise, it'll eat you up and spit you out.'

She lowered her hands, which had been holding the glass, and stared at him. Was he extraordinarily intuitive, she wondered, or did he actually read minds? She ran her tongue over her bottom lip. 'I'll make coffee,' she said, leaping to her feet and removing his plate quickly.

'I'd prefer tea, if you have it.' Nick also rose, following her across to the sink. His mouth turned down wryly. 'I almost gutted myself with coffee a while back.'

'And couldn't sleep, no doubt?' Melanie reached out for teabags.

'Didn't want to,' he clarified with a grunt of self-derision. 'I'd just been dumped.'

'Oh.' She waited and after a few moments he began to speak.

'Her name was Sonia Morel.' He seemed lost in thought, peering out through the window at the muted light filtering through the trees from the street.

'We were colleagues at St David's. Lived together for about a year. It ended.'

Just like that? Relationships usually wound down, didn't they? But, then, hers hadn't. Melanie let water gush into the sink and slid his crockery into the suds.

'She went back to her former husband.' Nick lifted his chin, the action emphasising the stubborn set of his jaw. 'He'd been in the Antarctic for over a year. Came back and they met up again. Fell in love again, she said.' His mouth twisted. 'She was gone within a week.'

Melanie kept quiet, sensing he didn't want pity or even commiseration. She handed him a mug of tea. 'Was that the reason you came to Murrajong?'

He gave a huff of wryness. 'It wasn't an easy decision, but my life was in limbo and Murrajong seemed somewhat of a challenge.'

Melanie felt her heart give a strange little flutter. Would it turn out a challenge for her as well?

'Lucky Murrajong,' she said, a false brightness covering a multitude of mixed emotions.

'You wanted to see the cottage.' He changed tack abruptly. 'What about tomorrow?'

'Tomorrow?' Her heart fluttered. Just the thought of spending time with him—getting to know him away from the hospital—was making her flesh tingle, her nerve ends zing.

'Mmm.' He gave her a look from under half-closed lids.

'OK, thanks. I'd like to,' she said, before she could allow herself to summon up a hundred reasons why she should keep some decent distance between herself and this complex, compelling man.

'Want me to pick you up?' he asked softly, making her insides feel as if they were floating away on air.

She shook her head. 'I'll be fine, thanks. I have my car back at last. What time?'

He thought for a minute. 'Anytime after two should be fine.'

A wry smile curved her lips. 'After you've finished dicing with death, I suppose.'

He cocked an eyebrow at her. 'You could always come out and watch me jump.'

'No, thanks!' She suppressed a shudder. 'I prefer my nails just the length they are. Why do you do it, anyway?'

He shrugged. 'The adrenalin rush, probably. It's almost as good as sex.'

Melanie rolled her eyes. If she'd heard that analogy once, she'd heard it a dozen times.

Amusement flared in his eyes. 'No comment, Melanie?'

'No comparison,' she countered, and flushed slightly.

'Ah!' He laughed and drained his tea, placing the mug beside him on the bench. 'I'll see you tomorrow, then.' Bracing his hands, palms down on either side of him, he leaned forward and brushed her mouth with his very softly, his tongue dipping briefly into its sweetness and then withdrawing. 'Thank you for dinner,' he murmured. 'And your lovely company. I'll see myself out.'

After he'd gone Melanie stared at nothing for

about two minutes, then shook herself, trying to direct her thoughts elsewhere—such as what to wear to Crafters tomorrow and why it should matter so much, anyway.

Melanie got out of the shower, still dithering about what to wear. Telling herself that the idea was merely to look around the old cottage and perhaps enjoy a tramp through its quite extensive grounds did no good.

Who was she kidding? she asked herself in silent disgust, throwing her softest, sleekest pair of jeans across the bed, while she collected lacy underclothes from the bureau drawer. Crafters was the convenient excuse, the catalyst to bring her and Nick together, and they both knew it!

With an effort she pulled her thoughts together and dressed quickly in her jeans and a plain, white T-shirt. What was the weather doing? She pushed her head out of the window and grimaced. A series of menacing grey clouds were gathering along the horizon, which meant rain. But, perhaps, not until later in the afternoon, she thought hopefully.

She blew out a calming breath and slipped on a plum-coloured long-line, ribbed sweater, smoothing it over her hips. Sliding her feet into neat little ankle boots, she caught sight of her reflection in the mirror as she straightened.

She gave a fractured sigh, picking up her brush and stroking it almost harshly through her hair. Get some sense, Melanie, she warned her flushed image as she tied back her hair with a soft multicoloured band and then, in a final dash of bravado, coloured her mouth expertly with a matte lipstick.

With her car newly serviced, she covered the five kilometres to Crafters in record time. As she parked outside the cottage she wondered whether she should have left home somewhat later. Would she appear too eager, too anxious? She bit her lip and took a steadying breath, noticing Nick's Jaguar parked beside the cottage.

At least he'd got home in one piece, she reflected, surprised at the surge of relief she felt. Pocketing her keys, she slid out of the car and began the trek up the long sweep of stone-flagged steps leading to the front door.

It was all quite lovely, she decided, her eyes feasting on the miniature roses and tumbling array of small perennials that bordered the walkway and spilled down into the roughly hewn rockeries.

'Thought you'd chickened out!' Nick had obviously been watching for her. He swung open the door with a flourish.

'It's only just past two,' Melanie defended herself, her gaze flickering helplessly all the way down his body and back up again. He was all casual grace. Even the brief action of opening the door had given definition to the interplay of lean muscles that rippled beneath the close-fitting jeans and pale grey sweatshirt. He dipped his head and smiled and she saw that his hair was still damp from the shower.

'I missed you,' he said barely audibly, and raised a hand to touch her cheek. Then he drew her inside, keeping his arm casually about her shoulders, and began to show her around the interior of the cottage.

'I boned up a bit on its history,' he confessed rather sheepishly. 'Found an old diary in one of the cupboards.'

'And?' Melanie couldn't stem the expectant smile that curved her lips. Her eyes were alight with interest as she surveyed the pine dresser, rag rugs and old-fashioned wicker chairs with their leafy-patterned covers.

'Built in the 1870s.' His mouth curved a little and he shot her a quick glance. 'And the original owners grew lavender as a commercial crop. Miss Donnington was the variety that thrived best, apparently. And you're laughing at me,' he said accusingly, a reciprocal amusement stirring in the depths of his blue eyes.

'No, I'm not.' Melanie stifled a giggle. Breaking from the warm, sweet weight of his arm across her shoulders, she held out her hands towards the gentle heat of the pot-bellied stove. 'I can't believe I'm actually here,' she said almost to herself. 'It's so charmingly *old*.'

'Old I can live with, at a pinch,' Nick said repressively, 'but I'm pleased to say the present owners have had modern plumbing installed plus an electric stove. Care to see the rest of it?' He dug his hands into the back pockets of his jeans, suddenly carefree, expectant, and she smiled back, caught up in his mood.

They peeped into the one and only bedroom.

'Like the brass bed?' He nudged her playfully with his hip.

Melanie shrank back as if she'd been struck. How could something as innocuous as a dark blue throw rug and prosaic blue and white striped pillows start her pulses racing?

'Authentic.' Her mouth dried.

Following blindly, she saw the rest of the cottage in a daze, and then he took her outside. Everything was rustic and wonderful. Her gaze wandered back and forth across the collection of old pots, sprouting all kinds of herbs and flowers side by side in happy confusion.

'Unless I'm mistaken, this is menthol mint,' she said in surprise, stooping to finger the light green leaves trailing out of an ancient, rusty bucket.

'As in lamb and mint sauce?'

'Of course not,' she tutted. 'It's medicinal. Sniff.' She broke off a leaf, crushed it and held it under his nose.

'Ah—it's clearing my sinuses already,' he said in a parody of a television commercial.

Melanie made a swipe at him and he side-stepped, laughing as he tipped a large, cracked earthenware pot with his boot.

'At least I know this is parsley,' he said knowledgeably. 'My mother has heaps of it growing on her balcony. She loves her plants.'

There was a small pause and Melanie threw him a questioning look.

'She's been on her own a long time now. My father was killed in a needless industrial accident when I was sixteen,' he explained in clipped tones.

She saw the heart-breaking bitterness that froze his features for an instant. 'I'm sorry, Nick,' she murmured. 'It must have been awful.'

Another cog fell into place—his white-hot, seemingly unreasonable anger against the timber mill's safety procedures after Steven Fraser's accident.

'Tom Cavallo was our rock, our anchor,' he said quietly. 'When I look back now I don't know how we coped.'

Her heart turned over. 'You're close to your mother?'

'Oh, yes. Ann's very special.' He shot Melanie a dry look. 'Always let me do my own thing, though.'

'Did you always want to be a doctor?'

He shook his head. 'No. I just knew I had to study hard at school so my mother would have one less thing to worry about. When my final year marks were good enough to get me into medicine, I went ahead.'

A gossamer-thin thread of awareness seemed to shimmer between them, draw them slowly together. Quite without thinking, because it suddenly seemed the most natural thing in the world, Melanie took the initiative and held her hand out to him, tightening her fingers in his and feeling him respond.

'Show me round the garden,' she said.

It was much more than a normal-sized block, Melanie soon realised. In fact, it was almost two hectares in area, a mishmash of native flora, metre-high weeds and introduced fruit trees.

'Hang on, Nick, I'm caught on this bush thing,'

she wailed, as they were making their way to the citrus grove at the rear of the paddock.

'You should know better than to go barging into wait-a-while,' Nick admonished, carefully beginning to untangle her from the bush.

'Is that what it's called?'

'Mmm. For the obvious reason. You have no choice but to wait a while until you disentangle yourself.'

'Oh, help! Even my hair's caught—'

'Hold still,' he muttered, fingering her temple. 'You've a long scratch here, you know.'

'Oh, dear! Have I?'

'Mmm. Want me to kiss it better?'

She tossed him a super-dry look. 'Some antiseptic when we get back indoors might be more to the point.'

The first, sudden drops of rain had them both craning skywards.

'Better leave the citrus for another time.' Nick grabbed her hand and began to tow her swiftly back along the barely discernible track to the cottage. When they arrived they were laughing and slightly out of breath.

'Are you wet?' Nick was all concern.

'Only a bit,' she said, hauling off her jumper and hanging it over a chair near the stove.

'Here, let me dry your hair.' He produced a fluffy towel and drew her down onto the big old chesterfield in front of the fire. 'How's that?' he asked, after a few minutes of gentle stroking.

'Lovely.'

'Come here...' Nick tossed the towel to one side and drew her against him. 'This has been the longest week of my life,' he said against her hair. His voice sounded deeper, huskier, seeking out hidden nerve endings, seeping along veins and right into her heart.

'For me too,' she whispered against his chest.

'I want you, Melanie...so much, so badly...' He spoke as if the air was being pushed out of his body.

I want you, too, she could have said, but didn't. Suddenly all her doubts, past and present, were back, closing about her like steel traps.

'Nick...' She drew back and looked at him, an odd little spiral of unease in her stomach. 'It's not that simple.'

'Someone else?'

'No.' She shook her head. 'Not like that. I'm just not sure...' She tensed and he narrowed his eyes slightly.

'Don't you feel close to me?'

Melanie faced him, with uncertainty and wariness clouding her eyes. 'I've been hurt...'

He turned her shoulders a fraction. 'I won't hurt you.'

'You can't know that.' Every detail of his hands was conveyed to her through the thin cotton of her shirt. The long, tapered fingers curved over her shoulders, the angle of his thumbs pointing inwards, their tips teasing the hollow at the base of her throat.

'I *can* know that, Melanie. I won't hurt you.'

It had been the longest time since she'd been held and never, she suspected shakily, quite like this. He kissed her then, the merest brush of his mouth over hers. It might not have happened at all, so fleeting, so exquisite, was the contact, but she was electrified.

Gasping, she wound her arms around him, her fingers riding the complex contours of his back as they slid under his sweatshirt. A wildness surged through her, like flames licking along a line of fireworks. This was good. Wonderful. And his body matched hers so perfectly...

'Melanie...' His hands went on their own quest, half circling her ribcage, driving upwards until his thumbs stroked the soft underswell of her breasts.

'Melanie?' Now it was a question, one to which she still did not have the answer. His breathing became more urgent and he eased her back onto the chesterfield, his mouth and tongue seeking the soft skin of her midriff. He tugged her T-shirt higher, then almost roughly pulled it back into place. 'What do you want?' he rasped.

'You...' she breathed.

'Are you sure?'

It took a long time but she finally said it.

'Yes.'

It was almost an hour later when Melanie murmured, 'How did we get here?'

'I carried you,' Nick said softly, and kissed her eyelids. They were in the brass bed, lying facing each other, with their arms around each other.

'Oh, yes. I remember now,' she teased, freeing a hand and running a finger along his jaw. She stared into his eyes and let her fingers drift into his dark hair, suddenly shaken by a rush of emotion. 'Nick?'

'Mmm?'

She buried herself against him. 'It doesn't matter...'

'Yes, it does. Tell me,' he prompted, stroking her hair.

'It sounds so trite.'

'Tell me anyway.'

'I feel so—whole.'

He seemed to give her statement long consideration before he said, 'It's a good feeling. I have it too.'

Melanie raised herself slightly and blinked. 'It's still raining.'

They dozed a bit and then woke.

'Was that my tummy or yours?' Nick rubbed his chin on her hair.

Melanie smiled. 'We missed out on our crumpets for afternoon tea.'

Laughing softly, he half spanned her waist with his hands. 'I have my crumpet right here.'

'Cheek!'

'That, too.' He grinned, sliding his hand lower. His eyes softened. 'Not regretting anything, are you?'

'N-no.' She bit her lip, not quite looking at him.

'Don't go away from me, Melanie.' He moved one hand, gently stroked the silken strands of hair away from her temple and then lowered his mouth to the pulse there. 'You disappear inside your head sometimes.'

God, she was beautiful, he thought. And so sensual. Renewed desire for the sweet fruits of her body burned a path from his mouth to the tips of his toes.

'Melanie…'

Her eyes focused, widened. She looked at his mouth, at the generous sweep of his bottom lip, and his eyes, the pupils enlarged but with the glitter of desire in their dark blue irises. The scent of him teased her nostrils, the rubbing of his skin against hers became heat-borne, electric. They belonged together, she thought, and this—this loving was right.

She began to touch him, as if something beyond her was activating her instincts, instructing her in actions she'd never made before.

Nick's jagged breath was like music to her ears. She felt his shudder and felt the victor. But with the thought came her own explosion of the senses. The soft sounds of mate calling to mate echoed deep in her throat as he claimed her mouth, and with a little sob she took him to her and reached for a million stars.

CHAPTER SEVEN

LIKE children, light-heartedly, they showered together, and Nick insisted on towelling Melanie dry.

'You're enjoying this, aren't you?' She sent him a somewhat indulgent, half-amused look.

'Aren't you?'

Of course she was.

'There you are. All dry.' He looped the towel around her and drew her close. 'You're not going home tonight, are you?'

Melanie shook her head. She could no more have left him than fly to the moon on the fold-away ironing board stashed against the wall behind them. She fingered the towel hitched around his waist. 'Do I get to dry you?'

He laughed and jumped backwards. 'Not if you want to eat tonight.'

Melanie was still chuckling to herself as she dressed again in her jeans and one of his big warm jumpers.

They decided to make omelettes—at least, Nick did. 'I'm good at this,' he said, when she peered over his shoulder at the worktop.

'What herbs do you want?' she asked, determined to be helpful.

'Ah...' He half turned and shot her a baffled look.

'You don't know one from the other, do you?' Her eyes held laughing disbelief.

He grinned, prevaricating. 'I do when they're in the supermarket and nicely labelled.'

Melanie laughed. 'Give me a torch then and I'll see what I can find outside.'

'Spare us the menthol mint,' he called after her, and she smiled until her face felt as though it might crack.

I could die at this moment, she thought, and know I'd never been so happy.

But by Sunday evening all her doubts had returned.

She and Nick were watching a movie on television, having spent a magical day together, and she should have been happy. So happy…

'Nick, I'm going home.'

He turned to her, a beam of light from the table lamp angling across the faint shadow on his jaw.

'Why?'

She coloured and said awkwardly, 'I need to, that's all.'

His eyebrows flexed. 'Is it my cooking?'

'No.' She gave a strained little smile. 'I've things to organise. My uniform to iron…'

Nick eyed her silently. 'All right,' he said quietly, 'if that's what you want.'

Melanie went early to work on Monday. Sean was the first person she saw. He sent her a dazzling smile. 'Nice weekend?' he asked.

'Lovely.' A burning flush travelled up her throat. 'You?'

'Tam didn't tell you?'

'Like a clam.'

'That's my girl. Ah—what have we here, young Melanie?' He eyed the plastic container she was carrying.

'Pikelets.' She edged in front of him into the staffroom. 'I was up early. Thought I'd make some for morning tea.'

'Hey, terrific!' He lifted the lid. 'I'll have my share now.'

Melanie tutted, watching him wolf down a handful. 'How on earth did your mother ever feed you, Sean?'

'With great difficulty, from all accounts. I'm out of here,' he said, replacing the lid carefully. 'Oh, the boss was looking for you earlier, Mel.'

Her heart fluttered. 'I'd better see what he wants, then.'

Nick was just coming out of his office as she approached. 'Looking for me?' Her smile faltered. He looked positively grim.

'I need to talk to you,' he said, his voice clipped and impersonal.

'Can't it wait? I have to take report.'

'Delegate. My office as soon as you can.'

Melanie hurried away, the nerves of her stomach gathering and clenching.

'Come in and close the door,' Nick said, when she got back to his office. He pulled a couple of chairs together and they sat, facing one another. 'Melanie.'

He reached out and took her hands, rubbing his thumbs almost absently over her knuckles. 'I have something to tell you.'

Her mouth dried. He was about to tell her he'd had second thoughts—that the weekend had been a mistake.

'Evie Dean died last night.'

'Evie…' Her mind refused to take it in.

'She collapsed at home.' Nick's hold tightened. 'Her neighbour called an ambulance. It was a slow aneurysm.'

Melanie paled and whispered, 'You mean Evie was ill, dying, while we were—'

Nick frowned. 'There was nothing either of us could have done, Melanie.'

'Well, you would say that, wouldn't you?'

'Why did I know you'd be like this?'

'Like what?' She barely controlled the accusation in her voice.

'Like we've spent the weekend doing something to be ashamed of.'

Melanie swallowed the tears clogging her throat. 'I used to call in on Evie of a Sunday—'

'And I'm sure she appreciated it.'

'Don't patronise me!' She snatched her hands away. 'If it hadn't been for you, I'd have been with her.'

Nick stiffened and went very still, the grooves of tension spiking his lean cheeks like slashes from a sharp-edged sword. 'I'll wear a lot of things, Melanie,' he warned grittily, 'but not that.'

'Not what?' Her head snapped up as if he'd clipped her on the jaw.

'Your morning-after guilt.'

Shaken, feeling trapped because he'd correctly diagnosed her muddled reasoning and had come uncomfortably near the truth, she rebounded on him. 'You said you wouldn't hurt me.'

'Doesn't that cut both ways, Melanie?'

There was a sickening silence.

Feeling ill and cold, as though all the air had been sucked out of her, she whispered, 'I felt so safe with you.'

Nick pulled air into his lungs and let it go.

'And I with you.'

He swivelled in response to the ringing telephone. 'Yes, what is it?' he snapped, scooping a hand through his hair as he listened. 'OK, thanks.' He put the receiver back slowly.

'Evie's sons are arriving from interstate mid-morning. Glen has left a message to be woken when they get here. Could you arrange for someone to go across to her quarters?'

I hate this, Melanie wept silently. It's all so final. She swallowed thickly. 'I'll go myself. What about Evie's cat?'

Nick looked frustratedly at her. 'Surely the family will take him?'

'Cats of Mendelssohn's age don't transplant very well.'

'Melanie, what is it you expect me to do?' he ground out, and then his phone rang again. He

stretched out a hand for the receiver and listened.
'OK, five minutes.'

As he replaced the receiver he informed her
tersely, 'I have an informal meeting with the board.
Get me out if you need me.' He stood and began to
shrug himself into his jacket. 'Look, I'll have the
damned cat, if it will take that martyred look off your
face.'

'Collecting strays again, are you, Nick?' Sick with
hurt and disillusionment, she couldn't hold back the
stinging barb.

Nick scrabbled some bits and pieces off his desk
and shoved them into his pockets. 'You're hell-bent
on screwing things up, aren't you?' In an abrupt
movement he bent and flicked her collar with his
thumb and middle finger. 'I should've kept you with
me last night, instead of letting you run home to iron
this. Who knows, this morning we may have been
still speaking the same language?'

Watching him leave, Melanie felt frozen. His back
was forbiddingly straight, blatantly shutting her out.

She felt a hundred years old. Evie was dead. She'd
hurt Nick irrevocably. Her insides felt tied in a thousand knots. She lifted her head and for the first time
noticed the roses. Nick must have brought them in
from the cottage this morning. Had he meant them
for her? Oh, Nick.

The real world could not be shut out indefinitely.
Melanie worked on in a haze of grief and disbelief.
Evie's sons, Greg and Patrick, came to the hospital
and she spoke briefly with them. Their mother's fu-
neral would be on the following day, they told her.

Their wives were presently at the house, packing up Evie's personal effects.

Melanie listened. She didn't trust herself to ask about Mendelssohn.

With determination born of self-preservation, she kept out of Nick's way, delegating everything she could.

Then the emergency call came, the outcome giving her no choice at all. Instead of avoiding Nick, she was running to find him and praying with all her heart they'd be in time.

'Where's the fire?' Nick seemed to look through her, his face a mask of polite attention.

Melanie swallowed the raw hurt. 'Possible arrest coming in to Resus. seven minutes from now.' She took a controlling breath. 'It's Ellyn O'Shea, Tam's mother. Cardiac history.'

'Is she on Lasix?' Nick's voice was clipped and they sped towards the resus. room.

'Large dose,' Melanie confirmed. 'Has been for some time.'

Nick looked grim. 'Possibly she's forgotten to take it. What could the ambulance tell us, Sister?'

'Acutely short of breath, clammy, cyanosed. Oxygen *in situ* and they've given anginine with nil effect.' Melanie's composure faltered. 'Tam will be devastated if anything happens to her mother...'

'Get a grip on yourself, Melanie.' Nick sounded impatient. 'Has someone got hold of the family?'

Melanie bit her lip. 'I'm about to do it now. I hope they're all where they should be...'

On her return they began to prepare the resus.

room. 'I'll check that.' Nick took the intubation tray from Melanie. 'I want you scrubbed and ready to catheterise. If she's overloaded we'll have to get that fluid off smartly. OK, Janey?' He gave the student a brief, encouraging smile.

'Yes, Dr Cavallo,' Jane replied.

'Good girl. I want the ECG monitor leads on as soon as our patient hits the deck, OK?'

'If she arrests you're number three, Jane,' Melanie reminded her. 'Do you know your job?'

Jane nodded. 'Write what drugs are being given on the whiteboard and help with IV fluids.'

'You'll be fine.'

'Someone alert Sean,' Nick said. 'We may need him.'

'He's left the hospital.' Melanie was scrubbing furiously. 'Having lunch with Tam somewhere. Must be out of bleeper range.'

'Brilliant!' Nick muttered.

'Should I get Dr Fielding?' Jane was already at the door.

'She's wiped out,' Nick said. He wheeled on Melanie. 'Suzy's still with us, isn't she?' At the charge's confirmation, he directed Jane, 'Alert Sister Parker. Tell her to stand by, then get back here.'

Jane ran.

Melanie felt her nerves begin to tauten as the wail of the ambulance rose and fell in the distance. It was like the overture before a grand performance, she thought starkly, watching Nick fling open the double doors of the resus. room.

Waiting.

Then there was no time to think.

'They're here,' Jane said, a little catch in her voice.

The ambulance backed up to the rear entrance, its doors already opening.

'Be good, team.' Nick's words snapped into the air, and Ellyn O'Shea was wheeled rapidly into Resus.

'She'll go any minute, Doc.' Bob Brand's face was grim. He'd gone to school with Ellyn.

'Not if we can help it.' Nick's hands moved like lightning, securing a tourniquet and IV in seconds. 'Sixty of Lasix,' he barked. 'IDC in now, please, Sister. Let's get that fluid off.'

Melanie sent up a silent prayer, blessing the months she'd spent in Gynae after her training. There were some skills you just never forgot.

'Bingo,' Nick murmured, as the crippling fluid began to drain out. 'Well done, Sister. Let's clamp it at eight hundred mil. Sixty of Lasix, please.' He bent to push the drug into Ellyn's IV.

'That's one-twenty of Lasix so far, Doctor.'

'Thanks, Jane. Could you turn up the oxygen to full now, please?'

Jane scrambled to adjust the mask.

'Ellyn?' Nick leaned close to his patient. 'Do you know where you are?'

'Hospital,' she gasped out. 'Am I going to die?'

Nick's hand rested briefly on her shoulder. 'Not this time. You've scared the daylights out of us, though. Did you forget to take your Lasix, by any chance?'

She nodded furiously. 'Gardening—forgot—'

'OK, one step at a time now. Just concentrate on breathing into the mask. Relax, Ellyn. Right—that's a whole lot better.' He shot an enquiring look at Melanie. 'How's the blood pressure doing, Sister?'

'One-sixty over a hundred. Pulse a hundred and ten, respiration thirty.'

'So far so good.'

Melanie saw his shoulders relax. He'd been as uptight as anyone, she realised. He'd just hidden it under total professionalism. What a shame they hadn't hidden their attraction for one another in a similar manner, she thought bleakly.

'Mel...' Ellyn's eyes fluttered open. 'Is that you, love?'

'Yes, Ellyn.' Melanie squeezed her hand. 'We've put out a call for Kevin and the boys. Tam's off to lunch. They'll all be here soon.'

The woman nodded and seemed to drift off. Some sixth sense warned Melanie that they weren't out of the woods yet.

'Thanks.' She took the basin and sponge from Jane and began to wipe Ellyn's face. She was still so clammy. Melanie frowned, and a terrible feeling of unease ripped through her as she felt for a pulse. There was none.

'Nick—code blue!' She hit the arrest button. Her gut clenched. Please, God, no! she implored silently, beginning to pump air into the lifeless woman.

There was a flurry outside and Suzy and Fiona appeared. Melanie issued orders.

'Tam's back,' Suzy enlightened the assembly, leaping to help with the intubation.

Nick swore. 'We can't have her in here. Has Sean got her?'

'In an arm lock.' Suzy's little face was fierce in concentration.

'Adrenalin ten.' Nick's controlled voice cut through the fevered activity in the room. 'And another ten. Any pulse?'

'No.' Melanie turned to him with fearful eyes.

'Let's defib., then, please, Sister.'

The room was suddenly filled with a high density of energy. As if by remote control, a pair of hands put the protective pads in place on the patient's chest and all eyes turned to Nick as he switched the defib. monitor to 'on'. The waiting seemed interminable while it charged.

'Clear!' yelled Nick. He tried once, discharging the paddles. No pulse showed on the monitor. 'Come *on*, Ellyn,' he gritted. 'There's a big wide world out there. OK, let's try again. Clear!' he yelled once more.

This time the gods were with them.

'OK. She's back.' Nick's affirmation was absorbed into the collective sigh of relief around the room.

Melanie slipped out quietly. Her nurses were more than capable of clearing up and preparing Ellyn to go to ICU. Holding a hand against her mouth, she took a short cut to her office. She shut the door and leant against it, then promptly burst into tears.

The rest of the day passed in a blur. Melanie cried herself out, muffled, gut-wrenching sobs that left her worn out and anxious. It was hardly the behaviour of a charge sister, she told her wan reflection in the mirror, proceeding to repair her make-up and straighten her hair. Only when she was sure she was under control did she venture back onto the ward.

Her shift seemed endless but finally it was over, and after hand-over she slipped up to the tiny IC unit on the second floor. Tam was just coming out of her mother's room.

'How is she?' The two friends hugged briefly.

'Stabilising nicely, thanks to all of you. Oh, Mel.' Tam's face worked for a second. 'What a scare!'

Melanie blinked, her teeth catching her lower lip. 'Let's sit for a minute,' she urged. 'Did they ever get a coffee-machine in this place?'

'And paper cups.' Tam palmed the wetness away from her eyes and gave a choked laugh. 'Trust you to be practical.'

'They're not sending your mum on, are they?' The young women made themselves comfortable on the cushioned window-seat in the visitors' lounge.

Tam shook her head. 'Nick spoke to her cardiologist in Brisbane. He seems to think she can be monitored here quite successfully. And she's better off here with all of us around.'

Melanie sipped her coffee and looked out at the landscape. Some of the trees, more suited to cooler climates, had still not lost their leaves. They stood out like sentinels, bristling with muted colour, sear and crisp. I've come to love this place, she thought. But how can I stay here now, with everything falling down around me...?

'I'm going to stay here tonight,' Tam said quietly. 'Ms Jorgensen has OK'd it for me to take one of the ICU shifts. I couldn't sleep if I went home, anyway. Mel—did you hear what I said? You seem miles away.' She ran her eyes over her friend's face. 'Perhaps you shouldn't be on your own tonight. What with Evie and everything...'

Melanie clutched her paper cup. 'I'll be OK.'

'We saw her yesterday, you know.'

'Evie?' Melanie's eyes flew wide.

'Mmm. Sean and I went to church. Ran into Evie afterwards. Actually gave her a lift home. She was having her friend, Mavis Tyrell, over to lunch.' A smile flickered around Tam's lips. 'She asked Sean to stop at the liquor barn and get her a bottle of decent sherry. She and Mavis probably had a high old time.'

'So she wasn't on her own?' Melanie's throat closed.

Tam shook her dark head. 'It was Mavis who called the neighbour. Oh, Mel—you didn't think—?' Tam put out a hand. 'Listen, honey, even if you'd been with Evie as usual, it wouldn't have made a blird bit of difference in the end.'

Melanie put down her cup carefully. 'That's what Nick said.'

Melanie drove home. Her mind refused to function, her head aching from too much thinking. Promising herself a long hot bath, she garaged the car and went inside. She had never felt so alone in her life.

The scented bath relieved some of the gloom. She

towelled off and dressed in her bright red winter robe, then wandered back to the bedroom. The quiet of the old house seemed to wrap around her and she lay on top of the quilt and stared at the ceiling.

The dull thud of the front door closing startled her. She sat up, drowsy and confused. Tam must have come home after all. Sliding off the bed, she peered out into the darkened hallway. Muffled footsteps sounded on the stairs.

'Nick?' She froze. His dark head came into view and then the rest of him. 'How did you get in?' She felt a mess, her feet bare, her hair tangled.

'Tam lent me her key. She seemed to think you might need some company.'

Melanie drew the edges of her gown together.

'There was no need to come.' Damn Tamsin and her eternal watching-over brief! She turned back into the bedroom, disconcerted when he followed her in.

'I was coming over anyway.'

She brought her head up, agitatedly pushing a long strand of hair away from her face. She was amazed he'd bothered. He'd looked through her for most of the day.

'Things got a bit derailed this morning.' Nick propped himself against the wall with his arms folded and his head angled towards her. 'We both said things we shouldn't.'

'Do we have to get into this?' Her eyes were filling up, her throat becoming blocked. Spinning awkwardly, she plonked herself on the bed, her gown swirling out to cover her bare feet.

'I think we do.' Nick's eyes remained steady. 'I'm

sorry about Evie, but there was no way I could have told you less than the truth. As for the timing—I probably could have handled it better. But I wanted to get to you before you had the clinical details dumped on you by the night team at hand-over. I really am sorry, Melanie.'

The soft apology was her undoing. She found herself blinking furiously. 'I'm sorry too,' she said in a low voice. 'And it's OK about Evie, I mean. She had a friend with her, when... I was just so afraid she'd been alone...'

Nick remained silent, studying her wet cheeks for a long moment. Then he leaned down and gathered her up, pulling her against his chest and smoothing her hair with long, rhythmical strokes.

'You're so special,' he murmured into her hair. 'So very special.'

She couldn't speak, the emotion of the moment overwhelming her like a tide.

But where did they go from here? she fretted as the tears began to subside. For the whole of the weekend he'd filled her thoughts like an addiction and now, against all good sense, she was back in his arms.

She felt his heart, strong and insistent, like the relentless beat of waves against the sand. His fingers stroked on. His breath was warm against her temple. I love him, she thought, acknowledging the fact with calm acceptance. But he was miles away from loving her. She knew that instinctively.

'I've been home and made dinner.' He pulled back and stared at her, his eyes assessing and then narrowing so that they resembled glittering shards of some mysterious metal.

'Have you?' At that moment dinner seemed inconsequential. She reached up to touch the pulse hammering at the base of his throat. 'Nick...' She made a little sigh of anticipation, her hips pressing against him in unconscious invitation.

'Melanie... Let's not make today any more complicated than it's been.'

Closing her eyes in defeat, she slumped back. She'd lost him. And she'd just offered herself to him, like a—*prize*. Colour scored across her cheekbones.

Her face set in a concealing mask. 'Nick, if you don't mind, I'd rather be on my own.'

'You have to eat,' he insisted. 'Why not eat with me?'

She shook her head. Food would choke her. Especially his! 'I'm not hungry.'

'Don't be infantile.' His steely gaze swept the neatly kept bedroom. 'Here, put this on.' He hauled out an emerald-green tracksuit from a pile of folded clothing and thrust it at her. 'I'll wait downstairs.'

'Don't you ever take no for an answer?' she demanded, aggrieved.

'Not often,' he informed her blandly.

'Don't bother waiting!' she yelled after him. 'I'll take my own car.' If that didn't show him she meant to salvage some kind of self-worth, nothing would!

'I'll wait, Melanie,' he called back. 'Get a move on.'

Gritting her teeth, she glared at the empty doorway, gave a despairing snort of laughter and began to dress.

CHAPTER EIGHT

'TRY this.' Nick handed Melanie a glass of musky red wine.

She took the glass carefully. Now that she was actually here at the cottage her courage was ebbing rapidly. Almost defensively she took a mouthful of wine, feeling its numbing effects on her empty stomach with ambivalence.

'Aren't you having any?'

'I'm on call,' he said. 'I'll make do with water.'

Melanie shrugged and, almost defiantly, took another mouthful of wine. 'Something smells good.' Banal comment, she thought wryly, but it was all she could manage.

'It's beef hotpot.' Nick removed the lid from a stainless-steel saucepan and peered in.

'Did you open a can?' Melanie shot the barb and then felt mean. He'd obviously prepared the food himself. Her nose had already picked up the tantalising results of long, slow cooking.

Nick grinned unexpectedly. 'Not a chance.' He reached up to gather plates from an open shelf. 'I made this last night after you'd gone. I knew I wouldn't sleep...'

Melanie flushed and stared down into her glass. His softly spoken words had been provocative, pulling her close again and wrapping her in security. If only...

'Enough!' she protested weakly, as he ladled another spoonful onto her plate. 'Although it smells wonderful,' she added, her antagonism dying like a candle in the wind. She was already a bit tipsy, she decided, very aware of the man so near to her in the confines of the tiny kitchen.

'Let's be slobs and eat off trays in front of the fire. OK with you?' He reached out and briefly caressed her cheek.

'Fine.' Melanie felt her breath cut off. Visions of their recent love-making tumbled through her mind, like so many snapshots quickly exposed and then suddenly put away. She didn't object when he refilled her wine glass.

The food was delicious and she told him so. 'Did your mother teach you how to cook?' They were almost at the end of their meal and Melanie forked up the last succulent morsel.

Nick gave her a very sweet smile. 'I mostly taught myself.' He looked thoughtful for a moment and broke off a piece of bread.

'Things at home had to change after my father died. Mum had to go back to work. She used to get home pretty late—at least it seemed late to a growing teenager with perpetual hunger. I began putting meals together so we could eat as soon as she got home. I did OK,' he said modestly. 'So then we began to plan simple menus and shopped for ingredients on the weekends.'

'I wish I'd had the chance to do that.'

Nick saw the lost little look in her eyes and wished he knew how to remove it. 'Coffee?' He stacked their used crockery onto one of the trays and got to his feet.

Melanie looked up warily. 'You're off coffee, aren't you?' She blinked. Two glasses of wine and she could hardly think straight.

'Tonight we're changing the rules.' Nick's mouth compressed momentarily. 'I'm having coffee and you're going to talk to me, aren't you?'

She shrank further into the corner of the chesterfield, not looking at him. His tone had sounded implacable.

They were halfway through their coffee when Nick said, 'Who was he, Melanie?'

She didn't even pretend to misunderstand his question. Her mouth thinned for a moment and she took a breath so deep it hurt. 'Aaron Prescott. He's a film director, up-and-coming, very charming, very focused and currently in the States. And I thought he loved me.' Suddenly, after all this time, it seemed a relief to spill it all out.

'Did you love him?' Nick's voice was soft like silk.

'Enough to want to conceive a child with him.'

There was dead silence and Melanie lifted her mug. It was unnerving to feel his eyes on her, and she thought how ludicrous the scene would appear to an onlooker. In one sense it was oddly domestic—until one felt the nuances. The male, with the shadowed face, the moody look, lounging back in his corner of the chesterfield. And the female, stiff with panic, despite the wine, trying to drink her coffee without revealing her shaking hands.

'Go on,' Nick said.

Melanie took a slow mouthful of coffee and kept her gaze lowered. 'What do you want to know?'

'Everything. For starters, where was your family when all this was happening?'

She swallowed. 'We're not very close. Like you, I'm an only child, but I had none of the nurturing you obviously enjoyed.' She grimaced faintly. 'My parents are both academics, very self-contained people. They were away a lot on lecture tours when I was a child. I was closer to our housekeeper than my mother. When I was twelve she had to leave for family reasons and I asked to go to boarding school. I loved it.'

'I can understand that.' Nick's face was averted, as he placed his mug on a side table. Nevertheless, Melanie could see he looked grimly angry. She straightened abruptly.

'Nick, it wasn't as though my parents were actively cruel to me. Maybe—well, with their career demands, they hadn't prepared enough to have a child.'

'They certainly didn't deserve one,' he rejoined darkly. For a few moments the silence was palpable, until Nick growled into the stillness, 'Go on with your story, Melanie.'

She stared helplessly at him. Short of walking out, there was no way to avoid answering him. And after the stress of a rotten day, plus two—or more than two—glasses of wine, she doubted whether she had the energy to move…

'When I was seventeen,' she recounted slowly, 'I went on my exchange scholarship to Japan. After that, and a careers night at school, nursing seemed something I could get involved in.'

'And you could live in,' Nick commented quietly, sensing her need for community living, for *family* of some description.

'Yes.' She nodded. 'Tam had come to Sydney to train. Our friendship began from day one. She took the mick out of everything, made me laugh. After we graduated we shared a flat for a couple of years. I met Aaron at a party…'

Melanie shrugged and gave a cracked laugh. 'I was hopelessly naïve. My unique circumstances meant I'd lived with my own gender for so much of my life…' She swallowed. 'I married him in a ten-minute ceremony one Friday night, spent a weekend honeymoon and then he was off filming again.

'We were happy for a while—at least I thought we were.' She stopped and put her coffee to one side. It was stone cold. 'When I found out I was pregnant I was thrilled. It—the baby—already seemed like a little person to me. I had days off so I decided to drive up to the Blue Mountains where Aaron was filming.

'To cut a long story short, it had been raining heavily and filming had been stopped for the day. Someone directed me to the caravan he was using. He hadn't even bothered to lock the door,' she continued bitterly. 'He was with his female lead…'

Nick heard the pain in her voice and clenched his

fists, as if he wanted to pound at something. 'I won't ask the obvious question,' he said very quietly.

Melanie laughed, a harsh tight sound that echoed hollowly in the quiet of the room. 'Please don't.' She couldn't bear to recount it even now.

She dragged in air and expelled it in a shuddering sigh. 'I hardly remember getting home. It was a tortuous drive what with the rain and everything. I started cramping in the early hours of the morning. I was in a panic. From force of habit, I rang Tam. She got me to hospital…'

Nick rubbed a hand across his chin. 'What's your situation now?' he asked carefully.

Melanie's composure slipped. 'Don't worry, Nick. You won't be dragged into anything unsavoury. We're divorced and I never told him about the baby.'

Nick's expression darkened ominously. 'Your former husband sounds like a rat, but it might have been beneficial, from your point of view, if you'd felt able to share the grief with him.'

She shook her head slowly. 'No, it wouldn't. And don't turn psychiatrist on me, Nick. I'm not your responsibility. Heavens—is that the time?' She'd flicked her wrist towards the light to peer at her watch.

Nick eyed her critically. 'You're in no state to drive, Melanie.' He'd heard the brittle note in her voice and there were shadows of fatigue under her eyes.

'Could you—? Would you mind?' She pushed herself agitatedly to her feet and he rose with her.

'Frankly, I don't feel like turning out—unless it's the hospital, of course.' He laughed without humour.

'But I can't stay here...' She hugged her arms around her, her teeth clamping on her bottom lip.

'Rats, you can't!' Nick was moving as he spoke. 'There's a divan-thing here near the window that folds down into a bed.' He ran his eye over her, as if he were measuring her size for the makeshift sleeping arrangements. 'What do you think? OK?'

'I suppose so...' Melanie stood numbly, her hand absently rubbing her arm. At least he hadn't suggested she shared his bed, she thought wretchedly. Away from the light, she couldn't make out Nick's expression as he got the bed ready, but her instincts told her it would be coolly detached.

Her heart plummeted. They were suddenly acting like polite strangers.

Nick busied himself, finding sheets, blankets and a pillow. Then he disappeared into his bedroom and came back with one of his shirts, a long-sleeved checked one. He tossed it to her. 'Modest enough for you?'

Melanie's eyes flashed. She took a deep breath. 'I could sleep in my tracksuit just as well.'

He shrugged. 'Please yourself. Do you want the bathroom first?'

She clutched the shirt to her. 'No. You take it. I'll do the washing-up.'

He looked exasperated. 'Melanie, leave it. Please.'

She lifted a shoulder in a helpless little gesture and sat down on the divan which was now a bed. A tear slid out of the corner of her eye and she brushed it away angrily.

Evie's service was strangely joyful. Melanie was still feeling the impact as she drove back to the hospital.

The children from the convent school had sung beautifully, a tribute to Evie who had for many years been on its teaching staff. And the priest had said that they were gathered to celebrate Evie's life. That had been a nice way of putting it, Melanie thought as a stray tear shimmered and fell. And oddly comforting.

Nick was right on her heels when she made her way back along the path to A and E.

'Uplifting service, wasn't it?'

Melanie spun as if she'd been shot, her heart contracting painfully. He looked darkly, superbly, handsome and very much at home in a well-cut charcoal suit, a crisp blue shirt and discreetly patterned tie.

'You were there?'

'Of course I was there.' He held the door open for her. 'And if you hadn't run out on me this morning, we could have arranged to go together. Over breakfast.'

She tightened her mouth and cast him a look that contained a mixture of sheer frustration laced with despair. She'd woken at five-thirty with a splitting headache, and all she'd wanted had been to get out of the cottage as quietly as possible and to get home to dose herself with aspirin and a long glass of orange juice.

'Were you hung over?' Nick's eyebrow quirked.

'I had a headache,' she dissembled.

'Oh…' His mouth turned down. 'Your bed not comfortable?'

'Perfectly,' Melanie said, calling up every ounce of her professionalism. If he was looking to get some kind of rise out of her, he was way off base. The normal smells of the hospital assailed her, making her feel slightly sick. 'I have to change back into my uniform.' She walked away quickly.

Melanie threw herself into restructuring the duty rosters with tight-lipped determination. There had been two more requests for shift changes for the upcoming weekend. Sighing, she juggled replacements and wished she'd kept her mouth firmly shut last night.

She knew now that the details of her past, her messed-up marriage, had been a real turn-off for Nick. She'd watched him mentally backing away by the second. Perhaps he'd seen it as a replay of his bitter experience with Sonia. Someone else's emotional baggage to sort out.

Damn! She stabbed her pen at the page and shaded her eyes. Her head still ached with a dull throb and her stomach resembled the residue from an all-night party.

'Sister—Dr Cavallo said could you come?'

Melanie looked up, focusing on Jane's scared little face in the doorway. 'What is it?'

'Spider bite.' Jane's eyes showed real fear. 'Ten-month-old baby. The mum's just rushed him in.'

Melanie jerked to attention, for the first time registering the soft keening coming from one of the treatment rooms. A surge of guilt stabbed her. If she hadn't been so self-absorbed she'd have heard the commotion and gone herself to investigate. Her mouth thinned. Nick had probably stuck another black mark against her!

She rounded on Jane. 'Is that the mother?'

'Um—yes.' Jane put a hand to her mouth. 'She's frantic. Her name's Farr. Kathy Farr. They're here on holidays, camping.'

'Right,' Melanie instructed. 'Your job is to get Mrs Farr out of the treatment room, Jane, but gently. And stay with her.'

'Yes, Sister.' Jane seemed relieved to have something positive to contribute.

It was all accomplished much more smoothly than Melanie had dared hope. Parents under stress reacted in different ways, not all of them helpful to the emergency care team. But Kathy Farr seemed to want to co-operate, even though she was obviously torn.

'Don't lose him...please...' she sobbed piteously, but allowed Jane to lead her away.

Melanie turned to Nick. 'What's happening?'

'Everything!' he understated cryptically. 'Jam jar on the bench.' He was using all his skill to hold the oxygen mask in place over the child's face. 'What the hell is it? None of us here can identify it positively.'

Melanie looked a question. Nick was rattled. Dear God! What if she didn't know? She took the glass jar over to the light and choked back her horror.

The spider was at least three centimetres across and deadly. In her old hospital in Sydney she'd seen what its bite could do to a grown man—let alone to an infant.

Her gaze flew back to Nick's. 'Funnel-web.'

'Antivenin?' he snapped.

'Should be in stock,' Melanie confirmed, tamping down her panic.

'Good.' His face lightened fractionally. 'Get it, please, Fiona.' He turned to the other third-year who was poised ready to run. 'And tell Dr Fielding I'll need her here, stat!'

Fiona ran.

Melanie moved closer to the treatment table.

'Where's the bite?'

'Finger. He's not looking good.' Deep concern catapulted into Nick's blue eyes.

Melanie's heart twisted. This beautiful little boy was fighting for his life. His small chubby body was thrashing and he was trembling, trying to breathe. The state of his plump little arm was already evidence of the spider's toxicity. It was beginning to swell, his skin an unhealthy shiny red.

'How much time do we have?'

'None.' Melanie took over the oxygen and Nick turned away to scrub. 'Children have died in less than two hours after a bite from a funnel-web.' She drew in a deep breath and then took hold of herself, smoothing back the little boy's blond hair with gentle strokes.

'Bingo!' Glen appeared, holding up the antivenin like a trophy. 'For a horrible moment I thought we'd come unstuck.' She raised an eyebrow at Nick. 'Want me to scrub?'

'Please. We'll dilute with normal saline. He's de-hydrating fast. And his veins are so tiny…'

A question hung in the air between them.

Glen scrubbed like lightning, letting the water drain backwards down her arms. 'Rather you than me,' she said in a quiet, very calm voice.

They debated quickly about the child's weight and decided on dosage.

'Nick!' Melanie's alarm rent the air. 'He's in shock!'

'Hold him!' Nick's reaction was instantaneous. The baby's eyes were rolling back in his head and he was beginning to stiffen. 'We need that line in,' he snapped. 'I'll have to do a cut-down for a vein in his ankle. It's our only option now—'

Despite working frantically against time, Nick's consummate skill made the surgical procedure look routine. But Melanie wasn't fooled. She knew just how much training it took to acquire such a delicate touch, a sureness that came only with long practice.

At last it was done.

'There you are, little man,' Nick said softly. The tiny vein had begun doing its work, carrying the life-saving antivenin to every part of the infant's body.

Even Glen Fielding seemed impressed. 'Not bad,' she understated, her small nimble fingers replacing Nick's to ensure the line was *in situ* and taped down.

'I was taught by one of the best.' Nick didn't elaborate. He pulled off his gloves and fixed Melanie with a steady look. 'I want someone from Paediatrics, stat. Jonathan will need monitoring for as long as it takes. We can't risk moving him while that poison is in danger of travelling.'

Melanie's gaze faltered and she frowned. When would he realise…? 'Nick, we don't have a paediatric department as such, only an annexe off the women's ward for non-acute cases. Anything else we send on to Brisbane.'

'OK.' His mouth twisted in wry acknowledgement. 'Then do we have someone with any paediatric experience?'

Melanie did a swift run-down of personnel in her head and stopped. 'Mike Treloar. He came here from a long stint at Mater Children's.'

'He's back and ready to work?' Nick turned away to wash.

'I've just done the rosters,' Melanie confirmed. 'He's due to start on a late shift tomorrow.'

'How is he? Have you spoken to him?'

'Briefly. He seemed fairly upbeat. Chris is doing well.'

Nick looked thoughtful as he dried his hands with brisk precision. 'Ring him, then, would you? Ask him if he'd mind coming in now. If he seems reluctant don't push it. I wouldn't want to load more stress on him on top of his recent trauma.' He turned to his locum and motioned for her to take over. 'Now, I really must speak to the mother.'

'Brilliant of her to have had the forethought to bundle up the beastie for us to look at.' Glen shot a questioning look at Melanie. 'I was under the impression funnel-web spiders were peculiar to Sydney?'

'They used to be.' Melanie went about quietly clearing up. 'But lately they've apparently been located in northern New South Wales and they've even crept across to us here, in south-west Queensland.'

Glen shuddered. 'In that case, I'll certainly be checking my bed before I climb in tonight. Poor little chap,' she murmured. 'Difficult when they're so vulnerable, isn't it? Makes me wish I had a magic wand.'

Melanie bit her lip. 'He will pull through, won't he?'

'Dear God, I hope so.' The locum's eyes were troubled.

Melanie avoided Nick for the rest of the shift. It wasn't too difficult, she thought with weary resignation. He was obviously avoiding her as well.

Hand-over went smoothly, with no requests for yards of additional information, and for once she left on time.

Taking the long way round to the car park, she eased her jaded spirits in the man-made rainforest on the hospital's periphery. Dan Nissen's green fingers again, she marvelled, drawn into its leafy, moist atmosphere.

Who'd have thought the lush tree ferns, staghorns and mosses could have been propagated here in this sometimes harsh climate? But Dan had managed it, even establishing a tiny trickle of waterfall.

Lovely, she thought, breathing in the luxuriant earthiness. Her gaze went out beyond the canopy of trees. There was still a low-lying mist across the ranges. It hung like a delicate bridal veil. Misty.

Secretive. Melanie stirred. She'd better get home. Life had to go on, no matter how difficult and awkward it seemed to be...

'Admiring the view?'

Nick's question snapped her back to reality. How long had he been watching her? 'Beats working on the rosters. Are you on your way home?'

'No, just out here for a breather.' Nick noticed her eyes were shadowed and faintly strained. He reached up and hooked a hand over a low branch of eucalypt. 'I want to stick around a while for Jonathan.'

Melanie met his eyes with a frown. 'He's stabilising, though, isn't he?'

'Mmm, but more slowly than I'd hoped.' He ran his finger along the uniquely pointed gum leaf. 'Let's say I'm guardedly optimistic. Thank you for persuading Mike to come in. He's good. Intuitive. And as you said, he seemed remarkably cheerful. Reclaimed his personal life, has he?'

Melanie shrugged. 'I believe so. They're getting a divorce.'

'And he's cheerful about that?' Nick made a rough sound of scorn. He pushed a hand back through his dark hair in irritation. 'I would've thought a failed marriage emphasised gross immaturity and a lack of guts on both sides to make it work. Not a reason to be pleased.'

Colour rushed to Melanie's cheeks. 'Then maybe he's pleased because it's finally ended. And it's just such a damned relief!' Fighting back sick resentment, she swung away and marched, stiff-backed, towards the car park.

'Melanie—wait! I was generalising. I wasn't referring to you!' he said harshly, following her.

'The hell you weren't!' Her eyes flashing, she shook off his hand. Snatching her keys out of her bag, she stabbed one at him. 'And what makes you the expert, anyway, Nick Cavallo?' she challenged bitterly. 'You've played around the edges, had affairs—but you've never *had* the guts to actually get married!'

CHAPTER NINE

'LET'S have a party,' Tam said. It was a Saturday and they were enjoying a delicious barbecue lunch in the back garden. 'Well?' She looked expectantly from Melanie to Sean.

'Great.' Sean's economical reply was muffled, and he finished off his third vegetable kebab with obvious relish.

'Why do we need to have a party?' Melanie's question was overlaid with unease.

'Because I think we deserve one.' Tam nudged Sean with her knee. 'Pass me the satay sauce, please.'

'Oh—sorry. These are good, Mel.' Sean placed the bamboo skewer neatly on his plate and reached for another kebab.

Melanie shrugged. She knew what they were up to. 'It doesn't take much effort to thread a few bits and pieces onto a stick. And I wish you two would stop trying to be so darned nice to me.'

The two looked like guilty conspirators.

Tam rallied. 'Mel, look, blind Freddy could see you've been on a bit of a downer lately. A party will do us all good.'

Melanie crumpled her serviette, looking doubtfully from one to the other. 'Who are we inviting to this party?'

'Not many,' Tam said airily, picking at a leaf of crisp lettuce. 'I thought a couple of the gang from Theatre. Jill and Roger, of course, any of the staff who were involved with Mum's care recently. Oh, and Mike Treloar. He's on the loose again.'

Melanie's gaze became shuttered. It was largely due to Mike's being 'on the loose' that she and Nick had had that short, lethal exchange of views. And now, two weeks on, there was still no sign of a truce. She stifled a sigh. She supposed she should be grateful they were still communicating—if one could call the tight-lipped professionalism they were both executing as communicating!

'In case you two are interested, I'm not inviting Nick.'

Silence.

'Mel, please,' Tam implored softly. 'This is way over the top. You have to go on working together.'

'No.'

'I'll invite him, then.' Sean dropped his skewer onto his plate. 'Poor bastard looks like he could use a bit of light relief.'

'Men!' Melanie blazed. 'You all bond together like some kind of mafia!'

'Hey!' Sean raised both hands, as if to ward off the vitriol in her words. 'I'm neutral.'

'You'll be *neutered* if you ask him here to a party,' Melanie promised darkly.

'For Pete's sake!' Tam twitched a long plait over her shoulder. '*I'll* ask him. He probably won't come, anyway. Now, let's make some plans. Next Saturday night OK with everyone?

'We'll have it out here.' Tam relished placing the seal on events. 'I'll ask Dad to knock us up a few braziers. Everyone likes a fire to gather round. Anyone you invite, ask them to bring a bottle. Mel, you and I will do the food. Oh—and I'll ask Gran to make one of her famous curries.'

Melanie showed a flicker of interest. 'Maybe we could make some tea-lights? You know, like we had at our graduation party?'

'Oh, brilliant! We'll need heaps of glass jars, though.'

'There's a whole box-full in the garage,' Melanie said, helping herself to some apricots from a selection of dried fruits. 'Remember, we found them when we first moved in.'

'Could I get a word in?' Sean shot them both a dry look. 'I'll supply the music, if you like.'

Tam looked at him with a pained expression and then grinned. 'As long as you make sure there's some good old slow stuff.' She leaned across and ran a light finger down the slight cleft in his chin.

Sean made a sound somewhere between a growl and a laugh. 'Trust me,' he said, trapping her hand and placing it against his heart.

Watching her friends, Melanie felt a lurching sensation of loss in the pit of her stomach. Tamsin and Sean had it all and their obvious joy in one another's company seemed like a symbol of all she and Nick had thrown away—if they'd ever truly had it in the first place, she thought miserably.

She stood quickly. 'I'll make coffee.'

* * *

Nick's car was in its space when she got to work early on Monday morning. It didn't mean he'd been called in, she thought philosophically. There was a quietness about the hospital she found reassuring.

Probably sick of his own company over the weekend. The judgement came involuntarily and brought her to a sharp halt as she opened the door of the staffroom.

He was sitting at the table, a cup of tea at his elbow and the newspaper spread out in front of him. He didn't look up.

Melanie went and put the salad she'd made for lunch in the fridge. 'Morning.' She turned and looked at him, a feeling of physical desire, urgent and unexpected, threatening to overwhelm her.

'The kettle's just boiled if you want tea.'

'Thanks.' She didn't, but she'd have drunk a dozen cups of tea if it had meant reclaiming a shred of normal conversation with him.

'Have you seen this?' He held up Monday's edition of Murrajong's bi-weekly newspaper, his eyes questioning.

Melanie caught her hands together and shook her head. 'Um, no, not yet.' Somehow she got her feet to move. 'What is it?' She bent closer to peer over his shoulder. Half the front page was taken up by a cheeky photograph of their little spider-bite victim, Jonathan Farr.

The caption said: 'Miracle. Brilliant work by Accident and Emergency team at Murrajong hospital saves young life.'

'Oh, my stars!' Melanie's fingers tightened on the back of Nick's chair.

'Make you feel warm and fuzzy?' He turned his head and smiled, and the terrible tension of the past two weeks vanished like smoke in the wind.

Melanie's heart hopped around in her chest. 'Quite a wrap for us—well, for you and Glen,' she said, bending closer to read the article. 'Why don't we send her a copy? Do you have an address for her?'

'Mmm. Should do. Nice idea.' Nick rattled the pages together and laid them down. 'If you've got a minute, I'll get it for you now.'

Standing next to him while he leafed through his diary, Melanie was sure he must hear the wild thumping of her heart and thought, It's now or never.

'We're having a party next Saturday night. Tam's idea, really. Just some nice food and wine. Outdoors. Very informal. Seven o'clock, if you'd like to come...'

Her little speech juddered to an uncomfortable halt. She closed her eyes and swallowed. And swallowed again. Damn the man! Why didn't he say something? Anything.

Nick kept his head bent. An intensity of emotion he'd never felt before gnawed at his insides. This time, he resolved, he would measure his response as if it were his last. He couldn't take a chance his words would come out all wrong again. He took a huge breath, held it and let it go. He'd thought he'd blown it with her. Had been sure of it. Thank God for olive branches in whatever form they came.

Melanie's fingers bit into her palms as she clenched them. 'Only if you're free, of course.'

'It sounds just what the doctor ordered,' Nick said carefully. 'Thank you. And thank Tam. I'll have to wait and see how things are shaping up in here, of course, but I'll come if I possibly can.'

Melanie whisked through the rest of the morning on a high. Even rechecking the procedure trays her third-years had prepared failed to dim her spirits. Still, she warned herself not to get complacent. She and Nick might have papered over their problems yet again but they had a million miles to travel to repair their relationship. Maybe the party...

Sean stuck his head in the door. 'You and his nibs kissed and made up, then? The temperature's risen about twenty degrees around the place.'

Melanie gave him a light smile. 'Very droll, Dr Casey. Can I help you with anything?'

Sean grinned. 'I'm looking for the boss man himself, actually.'

'Problem, Dr Casey?' Nick asked quietly from behind.

'Ah...' Sean went a bit red and touched the knot on his tie. 'I have a patient presenting with what looks like a ruptured Achilles tendon. I'd value your opinion so I can cover all the bases with the X-ray.'

'It's relatively open and shut,' Nick said easily. 'The injury is generally within the tendon sheath. Pain when the patient tries to plantar-flex the foot. In fact, the action is nigh impossible.'

Sean nodded. 'That would seem to coincide with what I have.'

'OK.' Nick pulled out his reflex hammer. 'I'll take a look anyway. What was the trigger? Sporting injury?'

'Sort of, I suppose. Sean looked uncertain. 'The patient was roller-blading. Came a cropper.'

Nick arched an eyebrow. 'A young kid, is it?'

'Ah, no. Not exactly.' The resident's mouth twitched. 'Fifty-year-old grandmother.'

'You're winding me up!' Nick looked questioningly at Melanie and she shrugged her innocence.

His deep chuckle was music to her ears. It was the first time in days she'd heard it. When the two doctors wandered off she found herself grinning like an idiot.

For the rest of the week she took nothing for granted, adopting an almost Zen-like philosophy of living life by the second. By Friday afternoon she'd dared to let her thoughts drift towards the party, wondering whether they should go the whole hog and hire a small dance-floor.

She was still sifting through the possibilities when Nick hauled her unceremoniously from a nurse managers' meeting.

'There's been another accident at the sawmill,' he told her in clipped tones, racing her back to his office. 'A workman's been injured. Trapped between his loader and a huge log. Bob Brand is there but the rescue could take a while. He wants us at the scene.'

Melanie quickly did a mental rewind. The scenario

Nick had drawn was laced with terrifying uncertainties.

'Emergency kit?'

'All done and in my car.' He was throwing off his white coat and pulling on a dark, ribbed sweater. 'OK, let's move!'

'Nick, I have to—'

'You don't.' His voice cut decisively across hers. 'The team knows the score and Suzy's been pooled to us for the rest of the shift. Just bring yourself, Sister, and some level-headed thinking. We're going to need it.'

'Direct me, Melanie.' Nick fired the Jaguar's motor and they shot like a silver bullet towards the main gates.

Melanie bit her lips together. She could tell, even without looking at him, that he was strung tight, focused…almost driven.

'You've been expecting this, haven't you?'

'I'll nail these bastards, if it's the last thing I do!' The words were softly lethal.

'Nick, it could be purely an accident—'

'Which way?' he snapped.

'Straight past your cottage.' Melanie was shaken. He'd already decided that the owners of the sawmill were culpable. Her hands found each other and interlaced tightly in her lap. 'Another fifteen kilometres further on we'll come to Skinner's Creek. Take the forest road on the left. The sawmill is a short distance from there.'

The sawmill was a mishmash of ramshackle buildings. The very look of them was enough to make Melanie's heart plummet.

'How can people be expected to work under these conditions?' Nick's face closed in anger as he drew in breath through clenched teeth.

'It may be just outward appearances.' Melanie's apprehension deepened. He looked angry enough to punch someone...

Nick ground the car to a stop outside a fibro shack that bore the sign OFFICE.

'Be careful.' Melanie's words were hushed yet they seemed to echo loudly in the close confines of the car.

His eyebrows shot up. 'I'll remember I'm a doctor first, Melanie, if that's what you're worried about? Now, let's find Bob.' He swung out of the car and began striding off towards a low-roofed shed, with Melanie almost running to keep up with him.

Bob Brand moved quickly to meet them, leading them over bits of rubble to the scene of the accident.

'It's grim.' The ambulance officer shook his head in disbelief. 'I can't imagine how Eddie McCabe, with his kind of work experience, could've got himself into this kind of foul-up.'

'Could be his tools of trade failed him on this occasion.' Nick's tone was scathing, his gaze, like a laser beam, going beyond the crew of hard hats over the chaos. 'What happened?'

Bob moved a bit uncomfortably. 'He was driving the end-loader, fork-lifting logs onto the platform. The forks jibbed on the last log. Wouldn't lift it any higher. Eddie got out of the cab to give it a nudge and, well, you can see what's happened...'

Melanie could, and was appalled.

Eddie McCabe's bright blue sweatshirt was just visible where he lay pinned between the relentless bulk of the loader's front tyre and a giant forest log.

Her fearful gaze ran the length of the log. After Bob's explanation, she could see now that the forks on the hydraulic lifting device had failed, allowing the log to roll back to its present precarious position. Several smaller logs had been forced down off the pile as well, and now formed an unsteady kind of teepee over the injured man. She went cold.

'He's been talking, but not a lot about how he is,' Bob was saying, and then they were joined by the foreman, who introduced himself as Darren Fritz.

'Right.' Nick frowned and tugged at his bottom lip. 'Let me get this straight. If we reverse the loader, the log is released and falls on Eddie. So, what are you doing about lifting the log?'

'We've got hydraulic jacks coming out from town,' the foreman said. 'But it all takes time.'

'Don't you have anything here for this kind of emergency?'

Melanie's head jerked up in alarm. Nick's acerbic tone would certainly rub the foreman up the wrong way.

'Er...no. Not really.' Darren Fritz kicked at a stone with his boot.

'What about the owners?' Nick was like a terrier with a bone.

The foreman shrugged. 'They live in the city. I doubt they'll come. They never have before.'

'We'll see about that!' Nick brushed him aside, snatching the emergency bag from Melanie's hand. 'Come on,' he said shortly. 'We can't hang about any longer.'

'Nick...' Melanie pulled uselessly at his arm. 'Nick...' She made another attempt to slow his stride. 'You can't go in there. I've looked. The log is balanced on only a fraction of its base and its weight is holding the others up.'

She might as well have saved her breath.

He squatted close to where the injured worker's feet were just visible. 'Eddie? I'm Nick Cavallo. I'm a doctor at the hospital. I'm going to help you.'

You and whose army? Melanie questioned darkly in her mind.

'Doc...' Eddie's voice was thin with strain. 'I think me leg's a gonner...'

Melanie's hand went to her throat. 'Nick...'

'This can't go on,' he said harshly. 'I'll have to get in there and give him a painkiller.'

'How?' She frowned. Eddie McCabe was caught so awkwardly that someone of Nick's size had no hope of negotiating a way to him with safety. She looked around desperately. The afternoon was drawing in, even as they stood there. And it was winter. Before they knew it darkness would fall, as completely and as quickly as a cloak thrown over the sun.

Eddie groaned again, the sound high-pitched and heart-rending, and Melanie's composure nearly disintegrated. They would have to do something!

'Nick, I'm going in there,' she said quietly. 'I'm smaller, lighter...'

For a moment they looked at each other and Nick swore under his breath. 'And what if the forks give way and the log topples?'

Melanie's heart lurched. It would be like a domino effect. 'It makes sense for me to go.' She pushed down her fears.

Nick's shoulders slumped as if he had no choice. 'We'll go with morphine,' he said tersely. 'Try to get the jab in his thigh.' He went to give her the drug then drew back. 'Melanie, I can't let you do this...'

'You can,' she said forcefully. 'You have to let me try.' Almost roughly, she peeled the ampoule out of his clenched hand.

'Hell!' The edges of his teeth grated. 'I hate not being in control of this situation. I hate it!'

Melanie sensed his anguish. 'Nick, I can do this. I took part in gymnastics right up to my late teens. I know about balance.'

For a long moment he looked down at her. Then his hand caught hers. 'Just so you know,' he said starkly, 'at the first sign of anything moving or creaking I'm in there, faster than a speeding bullet, to get you.'

'Hey!' Darren Fritz had realised what they were planning and jumped across the rubble to stop them. 'You can't let her go in there!'

Nick ignored him.

'Hey, I'm talking to you, Cavallo. You can't take over like this. The jacks'll be here soon—'

'And so might Christmas,' Nick growled. 'Look,

Mr Fritz, your worker is shocked and traumatised. He needs pain relief and we'll get it to him any way we can.'

'I've tried for better safety measures here,' the foreman said pettishly. 'It falls on deaf ears.'

'Then withdraw your labour.' Nick was ruthless. '*Strike*, for heaven's sake!'

Darren Fritz hung his head. 'They'll just sack us and employ others. It's a small community. The men need their jobs.'

Nick's lean, handsome face was stretched tautly. 'I would've thought they needed their *lives* more.' He turned abruptly and took Melanie's face between his hands for just a moment. 'OK?'

She nodded and steeled herself. From here everything was down to her. All her energies had to focus on getting safely to the injured man. She began to pick her way carefully through the rubble.

'Eddie? I'm Melanie.' She made her presence known calmly. 'I'm a nurse, Eddie. I have something for your pain. I'm almost to you now...'

There was room to manoeuvre—just. Melanie was conscious of toning down her movements, doing everything in slow motion. So careful.

To her relief, Eddie's pulse was strong if a little fast. She'd been dreading a different scenario, a rapid, thready pulse, indicating the possibility of a ruptured spleen.

Eddie's eyes fluttered open, dulled with pain but expressing all the uncertainty and vulnerability of his situation. 'G'day, love,' he croaked, and licked his lips.

Melanie began a simple test of his competency. His answers were strained but he got them out.

'You're going to be OK, Eddie.' Melanie was warmly reassuring, flicking her torch in his eyes, relieved to see his pupils were equal and reacting. Satisfied she could safely administer the morphine with no risk of destabilising him, she began to explain what she had to do.

'Eddie, I'm going to make a slit in your trousers. Relieve the pressure on your leg. It'll help your circulation as well. I'll be as gentle as I can.'

'OK, love...' His voice was barely above a whisper.

Poor man. Melanie held back her own distress. Eddie's right lower leg was wrecked. A *complete* fracture if ever she'd seen one. She'd have to administer the morphine—and quickly. Her face set in concentration, she made several quick cuts to the tough fabric of Eddie's trousers, exposing his thigh. Swabbing the site took bare seconds and finally she was able to shoot home the injection.

Melanie raised her head and listened, hoping for sounds of rescue, but there was nothing. She looked down at her patient. It would take twenty minutes or thereabouts for the morphine to work. She'd stay with Eddie, talk to him. Even though he mightn't be able to answer her.

There was no place as lonely as the bush at night, Melanie thought, and they were surrounded by it. At last the rescue had taken place and they were free to work on Eddie.

'It's been hours,' Nick said grimly. 'Heaven knows what his circulation's doing.' He drew the space blanket carefully to one side.

'What a crock, eh, Doc...?' The injured man's voice was a trace of sound.

'Stick with it, Eddie.' Nick was calmly reassuring. 'We'll have you out of here soon. Drip holding?' He glanced briefly at Melanie.

'So far. I had to feel my way in the dark.'

Nick grunted. 'Plenty of lights now, though.'

'Finally. The men even offered to rustle up a cup of tea.'

'Terrific.'

The brake lights on the ambulance glowed briefly beside them as Bob reversed and moved the vehicle closer.

'You're a surgeon, aren't you?' Melanie watched his hands, as sensitive to nuance as any violinist— palpating, checking, rechecking.

'Later,' he said, and lifted his dark head. 'You were magnificent, Melanie.'

'Oh...' She flushed, unsure how to take his compliment. 'I guess we make a pretty good team, then.'

Their eyes met for an intense moment, before each looked away.

'Right.' Nick seemed to collect himself. 'Go easy while we splint. He's had enough.'

'Hey, Doc?' Bob Brand's call was urgent. He jogged across to them, his wiry figure almost surreal in the dappled moonlight. 'The base has just been on to me. The CareFlight chopper can't get here.'

'Brilliant,' Nick muttered. 'What's happened?'

'There's been a bus accident on the Pacific Highway. Everything with wings within a hundred-mile radius has been requisitioned for the next couple of hours. The base'll send out the new ambulance and we'll take Eddie by road to Brisbane.'

Nick shook his head. 'We can't put him through that. Three hours on the road and then he'll have to wait to be assessed.'

'Well…two and a half,' Bob amended, 'if we slip into it.'

Nick looked down at the man's huddled form on the ground. He was someone's husband and some kid's father. And he was looking more vulnerable by the second.

'Get onto the hospital, Bob,' Nick said clearly. 'Tell them we're bringing the patient in for surgery. I'll need all orthopaedic trays sterilised and ready and at least two scrub nurses. Oh, and ask them to page Charlie Hunt to stand by to assist.'

'ETA?' Bob knew the voice of authority when he heard it.

'Thirty minutes if we work fast.'

Work fast they did. Ten minutes later Melanie watched the ambulance leave the scene, staring blankly into the darkness, her eyes following the tail lights as the vehicle dipped and glided over the rough terrain.

Good luck, Eddie. The silent wish came from her heart. She turned away, clutching the keys to Nick's car like some kind of talisman.

'Cuppa tea, love?' One of the men from the rescue team materialised beside her. 'We've made a brew.'

He pointed shyly to where the men were beginning to gather around the makeshift fire.

Melanie bit down on her bottom lip. This place was beginning to give her the creeps. Within seconds she could gather up her gear and be shot of it. But to refuse the men's kindness would be unthinkable. Bush lore, she reflected a bit ruefully. She forced a smile. 'Thanks, that sounds lovely.'

The eerie, high-pitched cry of a dingo from somewhere up in the hills sent goosebumps shivering along Melanie's backbone. She huddled quickly into Nick's anorak and hurried towards the comforting glow of the fire.

'You driving the doc's car back to town, love?' One of the men broke from the group and handed her a mug of tea.

'Yes, I am,' Melanie confirmed, and looked around her, realising she felt quite safe. These were good men. Some of them a bit rough and ready, no doubt, but as one they'd worked non-stop, slowly and painstakingly, to rescue Eddie.

'Better get away soon, then,' the man advised. 'Before the pubs shut. You never know who's out on the roads after that.'

Melanie beat back a shadowy unease. 'Dr Cavallo's left me his mobile phone...'

The man gave a grunt of dismissal, as though he didn't much believe in the infallibility of modern technology as far as the safety of young women was concerned. 'Tell you what,' he said. 'I'll lead the way in my ute and you can follow.'

Negotiating the bush road at night called on all

Melanie's defensive driving skills. The trees at each side of the road brushed past her vision. They were ironbarks, their gnarled, lumpy trunks resembling grotesque giants in the moonlight. A chill settled on her composure like a cold hand. She began to feel infinitely grateful for her escort up ahead.

When they reached the hospital gates her guardian angel watched until she'd turned safely into the car park. Then he tooted his horn in farewell and went on his way.

Mike Treloar was already waiting when Melanie parked the Jaguar in Nick's space. 'I've had someone watching out for you for ages,' he said. 'How rough was it out there?'

She shrugged.'Not that bad.' Now she was back within the safety of the hospital her fears began to recede rapidly.

'Here, I'll take that.' Mike took charge of the emergency gear and ushered her inside to A and E. 'Would you like a hot drink or something to eat?' he asked.

'No, thanks, Mike.' Melanie blocked a yawn. 'But I'd be grateful if you'd look after these for Nick.' She placed the set of keys and mobile phone on his desk.

'Sure. Anything else?'

'No…I don't think so. Oh, do you know if Tam was called in to scrub?'

'She was,' Mike confirmed. 'Ran through here like a whirlwind about an hour ago. Said to tell you she'll try not to wake you when she gets home.'

'Sweet of her!' Melanie tipped him a dry smile. 'But somehow I don't think I'd hear King Kong if he decided to come through the front door tonight.'

CHAPTER TEN

SOMETHING woke Melanie early next morning.

She lay, bleary-eyed, and listened. Subdued knocking. But from where? 'Good grief!' she muttered, and tumbled out of bed. It had to be at the front door. Was it a messenger from the hospital for one of them to report in? she wondered fuzzily. Was their phone out of order? Struggling into her robe, she made her way downstairs.

'Nick!' He was spectrally lit from the rear by the early morning light.

'Hello,' he murmured, his voice almost lost in huskiness.

'Has something happened?' Melanie clutched the edges of her robe tightly together.

'Can I come in?'

Her heart thumped. 'Of course.' When he was inside she closed the door and turned. Almost instinctively, their hands met and clung.

Nick exhaled slowly. 'Are you OK? I worried about you getting home from that dump.'

She smothered a shaky laugh. 'You didn't come here this early to ask me that, did you, Nick?'

'No.' He looked a bit sheepish. 'I woke so full of energy I didn't know what to do with it. And I thought of you.'

'Oh...' Her mouth dried.

'I'm going skydiving. I wondered if you'd like to come out to the field with me? I know it's early...' His thumbs caressed the backs of her hands almost absently.

'All right.' She didn't need to think about it. It was obviously important to him. Her heart began to pound, and for the first time she noticed he was already dressed for his sport in a maroon-coloured jumpsuit and thick-soled paraboots.

Her confidence wavered. His sudden appearance had filled her with a wild expectation, and she'd thought he'd come to— Well, what did it matter what she'd thought? He wanted her with him and that had to be a giant step forward.

Almost guiltily she unfastened his fingers and stepped back away from him, although her body ached to do just the opposite. To lean into him. To love him.

She swallowed thickly. 'Give me five minutes to change. Have we time for coffee?'

'I've a flask in the car.'

She nodded and started back up the stairs, unaware of his naked, almost hungry look as he watched her.

Nick took a step forward as if to follow her and then checked himself. That was not the way. The knot tightened in his stomach. He'd rushed her once. He wouldn't do it again. But it was hard—harder than anything he'd ever had to do.

Melanie washed her face and dressed quickly in jeans, bulky jumper and trainers. She picked up a brush and ran it through her hair, letting the strands fall where they chose.

I must have rocks in my head, she decided, making a face at her reflection in the mirror. Getting up this early to watch the man I love chuck himself out of a plane!

'You know, Melanie, you should try skydiving.'

'Nick...' She gave a little shake of her head. 'You're not going to nag me about this, are you?'

He lifted a shoulder. 'If you've done gymnastics, you'd be a natural.'

'A natural idiot,' she refuted darkly. 'How much further?'

'Not far. Five kilometres at most.'

Melanie pulled her cuff back and looked at her watch. 'Will we be home by eleven? I've stuff to organise for the party tonight.'

'Should be.' Nick gave her a half-smile. 'I'll be one of the first to jump.'

Melanie determinedly beat back the butterflies.

'Eddie's surgery went well, I take it?'

'It did, even if I say so myself. Of course, he'd be wise to stay clear of lightning strikes in the future.'

She nodded. 'A veritable ironmonger's store in his leg, I imagine.'

'Mmm. From now on he's a marked man.'

'It's probably better than being radioactive,' she joked. 'Where did you do your surgical training?' Her gaze went to his hands on the wheel and the question was out before she could retract it.

'Three years at John Bosco's in Melbourne. After that I spent a year in the States and I was in my second year on the surgical staff at St David's.'

'Impressive. Will you go back to St David's?' Melanie wanted desperately to know even if her heart plummeted at the prospect. But the day would inevitably come when his contract at Murrajong would run out and he would no longer be in her life—

'No.'

She swallowed. 'What will you do, then?'

His eyes flicked to her. For some reason they looked bluer and darker. 'I don't see I have to do anything yet,' he said. 'I'm contracted to Murrajong, and unless they've changed the goalposts and haven't told me I still have six weeks of my contract to fulfill.'

Six weeks. Her heart cartwheeled and she looked away quickly.

The sun had risen by the time they arrived at the airfield, a brilliant burst of gold-tipped fingers spanning the horizon.

'What a beautiful country we live in.' Nick placed an arm around her shoulders and held her to him.

Melanie drew in a shaky breath. It seemed the magic of the early morning had enthralled them, bound them in some way. Turning to her, Nick raised a hand and brushed a strand of fair hair away from her face.

'I'll just go across and see the lads for a minute,' he told her gently. 'And then we'll have that coffee.' He handed her his keys. 'There's a rug in the boot and food in my backpack.' He released her and walked away towards the hangars.

Watching him, Melanie shook her head, not able

to come to grips with a grown man's fascination for wanting to fly like a bird.

She had placed the rug on the ground and had their impromptu picnic set out when Nick came sauntering back. He lowered himself and sat cross-legged beside her.

'Forty-five minutes,' he said matter-of-factly.

'Until you go up?' Melanie frowned up into the sunlight, her heart sinking into her boots.

'Hey,' he remonstrated, chucking her under the chin playfully. 'I'll come back down.'

She felt the panic mounting in her throat. 'I...got the stuff out of your backpack.'

'Oh, good. Let's eat. Do you like blueberry muffins?'

'They're still warm,' she said in surprise, as she folded back the foil wrapping. 'Don't tell me you were up early, baking? Not that I'd be surprised if you were!' she added with a heavy touch of irony.

Nick's throat arched back and he laughed. 'From freezer to microwave. Does that qualify?'

'Nick...?' Melanie brushed a crumb from her mouth and kept her head bent.

'What is it?' He was taking slow mouthfuls of his coffee and looking into the distance.

She looked up slowly. 'When you jump or, more precisely, when your parachute opens...'

'Yes?'

'Well, surely, there has to be some kind of shock to your body?'

Nick studied her in silence for a long moment.

'You're really uptight about this, aren't you?'

'Anyone with a grain of knowledge about anatomy would be!' She lifted her shoulders in anguish. 'I don't want to have to gather you up in pieces…'

'For crying out loud!' He swung sharply to face her, his jaw jutting almost aggressively over the collar of his polo-necked jumper. 'Melanie, listen to me.' He caught her hand and looked at it for a moment and then laced his fingers through hers, almost as if he had to touch her physically to explain his point.

'I'm listening.' She swallowed. Her hand looked so small in his.

'OK, then. Admittedly, when the chute opens the parachutist's speed is reduced dramatically. If I'm dropped at, say, two hundred kilometres per hour, I'm cut back to maybe twenty in about two or three seconds.'

'My God, Nick!' Melanie shuddered. 'What does that do to your spine?'

He shrugged. 'There've been countless tests done. Physically, there appears to be no damage at all or so slight that it's infinitesimal.' He drained his coffee. 'More parachutists are injured in landing. Stop worrying!' He tried to make a joke of it. 'I'm the original cat.'

Melanie watched him dig into his pocket for his altimeter and strap it on his wrist. 'Why do you wear that?' Even with his explanation, the hard knot in her stomach refused to go away.

'It will tell me how far I can free-fall before I pull the ripcord.'

'What if you black out?'

'Hypoxemia? I won't be at a high enough altitude for that to be a possibility.'

'But what if you did?' Melanie was not about to be put off.

'Then the chute will open automatically when I've descended to a given height.' Nick got to his feet and pulled her up with him. 'Come on over and meet Gordon Bell. He's co-ordinating the jumps today. You can drive out to the pick-up point with him and he'll explain exactly what's happening.'

'That's presuming I want to know,' she qualified thinly.

His eyebrows rose. 'Don't you want to be there when I land?'

'Nick—'

'It's better than being here on your own and fretting, Melanie. Hey.' He cocked his head interrogatively. 'Didn't I once hear you mutter something about people being fearful in their ignorance?'

She made a face at him. 'OK, wise guy, you win. But don't expect me to like it!'

Gordon Bell was a man in his fifties, broad and solid and very sympathetic to Melanie's fears. She felt reassured, instantly at home with him.

'Nick will be among the first group to jump,' he told her, his faint Scots burr falling gently on her ears and somehow lulling her anxiety. That was until Nick came towards them, wearing his parachute and carrying a special helmet and gloves.

Melanie's insides heaved crazily.

'Cheer up, lass,' Gordon Bell admonished softly. 'It won't be much fun for him if he knows you're here on the ground, mentally biting your nails, now, will it?'

'You OK?' Nick stood in front of her.

'I guess this isn't where I say break a leg, is it?' She forced herself to joke.

He smiled briefly and touched her cheek with the tip of his glove. 'See you soon. Take care of her, Gordon.'

Gordon ushered her into a battered army-type Jeep and they drove at a leisurely pace over the flat, frost-browned ground for several kilometres to the pick-up site.

When they stopped, Melanie looked up. The small plane was already airborne, a dot in the clear blue of an endless sky. The conditions were perfect for sky-diving, she told herself. Nothing would go wrong. She even managed a fairly normal smile when Gordon handed her a pair of binoculars.

'You'll be able to see your man all the way down with these,' he told her.

Was he her man? Something twisted inside her. She had only another six weeks to find out.

'OK,' Gordon said, heaving his bulk out of the Jeep. 'The plane should be banking about now.'

Melanie scrambled out after him and put the bin-oculars to her eyes. 'How will I know which one is Nick?'

Gordon tracked the space with his own set of bin-oculars. 'Today, he's the only one wearing red,' he explained simply.

Red reminded her of blood. Oh, God! Stop!

'There he is now!' Gordon's voice rose excitedly. 'First one out.'

'Where?' Gordon, where—?' Melanie could see only infinite blue sky.

Patiently, Gordon swivelled her arms and steadied them. 'There,' he said. 'Can you see him?'

'Yes.' Her heart flipped. 'Oh, my God, he hasn't pulled his ripcord!'

'He will now,' Gordon said confidently. 'See, there it goes.'

'Oh, it looks like a pear,' she said in surprise.

'It inflates from the top down. Air fills the apex first, then expands the canopy from there down. See? It's *breathing* now. And now it's right open.'

'Ooh…it's beautiful!' Melanie was almost sick with relief. With her eyes glued to her binoculars, she followed Nick's slow, graceful descent from the heavens. She swallowed the lump in her throat. 'How does it feel, Gordon—when you're up there?'

'Fantastic,' he said, with something like envy in his voice. 'Magic. You're enveloped in utter silence. It's profound. Like nothing else you'll ever experience. Except maybe in the Antarctic. Watch now, he's coming in.

'This is most critical.' Gordon slanted his binoculars and edged closer to her, almost touching her elbow. Melanie tensed involuntarily.

'What if he messes it up?'

'He won't,' Gordon said confidently. 'That's it, Nick, lad,' he murmured. 'Watch now, he'll strike the ground first with the balls of his feet. His knees are slightly bent, see? And now he'll go into a roll

and throw his legs to the opposite side. Purr-fect!'
Gordon beamed at her, his teeth bared in huge white
tombstones of delight.

Melanie licked a salty tear off her lips. 'Can I go
over to him?'

Gordon touched her briefly on the shoulder. 'Of
course you can, lass. Run on.'

Melanie ran.

Melanie's outfit was new, a silk and wool two-piece,
comprising a slinky fitted top and long skirt.

Her heart fluttered as she stood in front of the mirror. Black had always suited her. She lifted a hand
and touched the tiny pearl button at the open neck
of the top. Its cropped style left a tantalising strip of
bare skin around her midriff.

She moved a bit, swaying in front of the mirror.
Her long skirt was heavenly, just touching the tops
of her new block-heeled pumps.

'"I could have danced all night,"' she sang softly,
and grimaced at her fanciful assumption. She still
had no idea whether Nick could, in fact, dance.

By eight o'clock Melanie was convinced Nick
wasn't coming and said as much to Tam.

'He'll be here,' Tam insisted. 'Trust me, Melanie.
I know about these things. OK.' She whirled away
like a small exotic butterfly in her oriental, red silk
pyjamas. 'Five more minutes and we start shoving
this food out. They've all had time enough to mingle
or whatever.' She frowned slightly. 'Music's not too
loud, is it?'

Melanie shook her head. 'I wouldn't think so.' She

peered out into the party scene beyond the kitchen window. Some of their guests were clustered in friendly fashion around the fires, while others, well into the spirit of the evening, were dancing light-heartedly to the music from Sean's sound system. 'I had no idea we'd asked so many.'

Tam made a small moue. 'What can you say when they ask to bring a friend? By the way, who's Mike's classy woman? He hasn't wasted any time.'

Melanie chuckled. 'You mean I actually know something you don't?'

Tam poked her tongue out. 'Well, who is she, then?'

'Phoebe Lyons.' Melanie took a mouthful of her drink. 'Chris's science teacher at the high school. I believe she's now a regular visitor to the burns unit at the Royal.'

'Oh...that's the connection! Bit young for Mike, isn't she? Are they an item, or what?'

'They're holding hands, if that tells you anything.'

The enlightenment came from behind and both young women spun around almost guiltily.

'Sean!' Tam made a face. 'Don't sneak up on me like that. And Nick!' She cranked her gaze higher. 'Hi. Oh, yum!' She accepted the bottle of coffee liqueur he handed to her. 'Madam here had just about convinced herself you wouldn't show.'

'For shame.' Nick went over to Melanie and brought her hand to his lips. 'And there I was just trying to turn an honest dollar at the hospital. You look beautiful,' he added in a husky undertone.

'Thank you.' Her heart was racing and she was

sure she was blushing. He was being outrageous—and wonderful. She drew in a long ragged breath. 'How's Eddie?'

'For Pete's sake, you two!' Tam rolled her eyes heavenward. 'No shop talk. At least not in my hearing.'

'When's the grub up?' Sean made an elaborate show of massaging his stomach. 'I could eat a horse and chase the rider.'

Tam giggled. 'Freaky!'

'Especially if you were the rider.' Melanie dodged a flying teatowel and came up laughing.

'You're looking very pensive,' Nick observed.

Melanie took a mouthful of her coffee. 'I was just wondering if I'd mingled enough.'

'You have,' he said determinedly. 'Besides, I want you to myself for a while.'

She lifted her head, breathing in the crisp night air. The tea-lights were sending out shards of colour from within their glass containers, and the lanterns they'd hung in the trees had conjured up a misty, magical ambience.

'It's been a nice party, hasn't it?'

'Brilliant,' Nick said.

They continued to drink their coffee in silence.

'Had you actually been at the hospital tonight?'

Nick turned to her, soft amusement in his eyes.

'Are we talking shop?'

'I—just wondered how Eddie is doing.' Melanie fiddled with her spoon. Despite the party and the cheerful crowd, the risks she'd taken yesterday had only just begun to hit home.

'He's still pretty groggy,' Nick said. 'All his vital signs are good, though.' He stretched out his arm along the back of her chair. 'I met his wife and young daughter this evening. They were visiting with him.'

'Are they OK?' Melanie let her body relax into the curve of his arm.

'Understandably upset at the battering he's taken. But at least they still have him, don't they?' He gave her a brief smile, sadder than it had any right to be.

'Oh, Nick...' He was thinking of his father, of course. Would it ever get better for him?

'The sawmill's owners,' Melanie broached carefully. 'I can't imagine you're going to let it rest.'

'Bet on it!' Nick took her hand and kissed it on the way to his lap. 'I've been on to the local MP. There'll be a team of government safety inspectors out there on Monday.'

'Will they close the mill down?'

'Not if the owners are prepared to bring it up to acceptable safety standards.'

'And if they don't?'

Nick looked grim. 'They'll face a hefty fine in any case—maybe even criminal charge for negligence.'

'And the men's jobs?' she asked helplessly.

Nick's mouth tightened. 'Melanie, all that can be sorted out later. I couldn't close my eyes to what I saw.'

'No...' Of course he couldn't. But surely there had

to be an alternative to fifteen men, most of them the sole breadwinners of their families, losing their jobs.

'Did you lace this coffee with brandy?' He lifted their clasped hands and set their elbows closely together on the table-top.

Melanie smothered a giggle. 'Are we about to arm-wrestle?'

'Cute!' His mouth touched her knuckles.

'I thought so. Tam made the coffee,' she dissembled.

'Oh. Do you suppose she was trying to loosen us up?'

Melanie snorted softly. 'She's like God—moves in mysterious ways.' She smoothed her palm over the raised cable-knit of his jumper. 'Soft...'

'Mmm. Alpaca wool. My mum knitted it.' He trapped her hand against his chest.

'I can't knit,' she confessed dreamily, and felt his smile on her skin.

'Neither can I.'

For a long while they were silent, then he sighed and Melanie opened her eyes.

'What?'

'They're playing our song.'

She looked at him, startled. 'We don't have a song.'

'We do now. Dance with me.' He scraped his chair back roughly over the lawn and pulled her upright.

In the shelter of the trees they could have been the only two people in the world. Her hands went up around his neck and his hands found their way to the bare, silky skin at her waist. A slow, soft ballad throbbed into the night air.

'Now I know,' she said.

'What do you know?' he murmured into her hair.

'That you can dance.'

He gave a huff of dissent. 'We're just moving to the rhythm. We always have done.'

But they'd got out of step more than once, she reflected soberly, and looked up at him. Her heart quickened. His gaze was heavy-lidded, intense, partly shadowed by the leafy canopy.

'Melanie...' His shuddering breath licked across her temple. 'Come home with me tonight. I need you...'

Her breathing faltered, almost stopped. It was what she'd ached for, longed for. To be part of his life again. Yet something held her back. She *loved* him. He *needed* her. And perhaps therein lay the difference.

He gave a sharp sigh. 'Don't start putting labels on everything, Melanie.' He was reading her mind again. As if he'd sensed her confusion, he bent, his mouth touching a river of tiny kisses to her throat.

'The future's not set in concrete. Do we let the present, when everything is fine between us, slip away in the meantime?'

Put like that, her reasoning sounded a bit pathetic. She buried her face in his chest and clung to him.

'OK?' he asked softly.

After a minute she nodded. 'OK.'

He took her hand and led her out from under the

old elm tree. 'You look like you're walking to your doom,' he joked.

'I don't, do I?'

'Just a bit.' His long arm snaked out around her shoulders, hugging her to him. 'Do you want to tell Tam we're leaving?'

Melanie blinked, hesitated. 'All right.'

'He's nuts about you,' Tam said with a satisfied little grin. 'Have fun. Sean'll help me clear up here.'

'Oh, Tam... I...'

'Melanie!' Tam said warningly. 'Just go.'

Nick's heart was trampolining as he pulled up at the cottage. He'd forgotten what it felt like to have these gut-wrenching feelings about a woman—or perhaps he'd never truly experienced them. That electrifying thought caused his nerve ends to pinch, screwing his muscles tight. He avoided touching Melanie. Instead, he opened the front door and waited for her to go inside.

Melanie looked around her, feeling an unexpected tightening in her stomach. She'd thought never to set foot in this place again. Not after the last time. Nerves attacked her, causing her to move jerkily, as if her limbs were controlled by strings.

Touching her hand to the wall of river stone, she looked back at Nick in surprise. 'It's warm!'

'Mmm. I lit the stove before I went out.' A couple of heartbeats. 'Melanie?'

The catch in his voice told her everything she needed to hear. She went to him and he caught her. Held her.

'We could put on some music and dance properly.' His hands moved down over her hips, rocked her gently.

Melanie's body flirted with his in a new kind of confidence. Her hands slipped under his jumper, finding his warm skin. 'Or…we could go to bed…'

He caught her wrist with his hand and pulled her closer. 'Or we could do both.'

They did and it was tumultuous, a landslide of feelings, a kaleidoscope of emotions, which they greedily harnessed.

Melanie had thought nothing could have been as wonderful as their first time together. She'd been wrong.

Nick's masculine power was unassailable yet she felt neither engulfed or put down. She shivered as he caressed the flare of her hips, the curve of her buttocks. She sighed when his hands became a cradle for her breasts and lingered as if they could never get enough. And then his mouth took over, tantalising her until she could stand no more.

Nick took her with him, his body the spur for her own wildness. And beneath him Melanie relished the weight of her lover's body. The giving-up was for both of them. Mutual. Making them one.

'Who said making up was hard to do?' Melanie's smile was slightly smug. She teased a path along Nick's chest with her fingernail and thought she could easily become addicted to his brass bed.

'Anyone who's had to do it,' Nick snorted. 'It's taken us days of frustration and heartache to get back to this point, sweetheart. Or had you forgotten?'

'No...' She looked at him soberly in the muted light from the bedside lamp. She hadn't forgotten.

His mobile rang and they groaned in unison. While Nick flipped it up and spoke, Melanie made herself comfortable beside him.

'I take it that was the hospital?' She shot him a sympathetic look.

'Mmm. Night sister on surgical. Eddie is in some discomfort. She had a query about the pain relief I'd written up for him.'

'Do you have to go out?'

'In.'

'What?' She squeaked as he scooped her up and brought her down on top of him.

'I don't have to go anywhere,' he said softly. 'Fancy another round?'

Melanie tutted. 'You're insatiable. Go to sleep.'

'Boring.'

'But necessary. I'll still be here in the morning.'

'It's morning now.'

'Nick—'

'I'm asleep.'

CHAPTER ELEVEN

MELANIE looked at her desk calendar and frowned. Nick's contract had barely two weeks to run and she still hadn't a clue where their relationship was heading.

He'd wanted her to stay at the cottage with him, but she'd vetoed that. Nevertheless, they were still spending every moment of their off-duty time together.

Her heart turned over. At least there were no signs he'd started packing. But when he did what could she say? Can I come with you? Fat chance!

The wail of an ambulance shot her back to reality.

The emergency concerned a student from the high school. According to the accompanying teacher, the child had suffered a seizure.

'Let's make her more comfortable, Jane.' Melanie couldn't help feeling sympathy for the youngster. Passing out in front of your peers would be a terrible embarrassment for an adolescent to handle.

'Poor kid,' Jane said quietly, easing off the girl's trainers and placing them neatly under the bed. 'She'll probably feel like the pits when she comes around.'

'Well, we're here to see she doesn't,' Melanie said firmly, stroking the baby-soft fair hair away from the girl's face. 'Would you get Dr Cavallo now, please? This is one for him, I think.'

Melanie had just finished getting the details when Nick pushed through the doors to the treatment room.

'Right, Sister,' he said briskly. 'Do we have a name?'

'Bronte Miller, aged fifteen.'

Nick began a careful examination of the child's head. 'Has she come around at all?'

'Briefly in the ambulance and lapsed again.'

'And she's been diagnosed epileptic?'

Melanie nodded. 'The school was notified recently.'

'Well, there are no obvious bumps.' Making his own observations, Nick was quick and thorough. 'Where did she fall?'

'On the oval.' Melanie secured a drip and taped it down. 'The girls were about to begin their usual PE session.'

'Probably very fortunate she didn't fold on the quadrangle, then.'

The child moaned and her eyelids fluttered.

'Coming back to us, Bronte?' Nick asked gently, and bent closer to the child. 'No? OK, sweetie, sleep it off…' He straightened abruptly towards Melanie. 'Let's get some blood. We'll test her dilantin levels. That might tell us the story.'

Melanie looked at him. 'Her GP might be able to throw some light on what's happened. What do you suspect?'

Nick looked thoughtful. 'I'm just wondering if our

little friend here has been despatching her tablet to someplace else other than her mouth.'

'Do you think she's in denial?' Melanie's brows rose.

'It happens. Pretty girl, popular. Sees the diagnosis as a death blow to her social acceptance.'

'Oh, poor kid.'

'Bronte's mum's here.' Jane popped her head around the door.

'Good.' Nick turned sharply to Melanie. 'Give her a couple of minutes with the child, then ask her to come to my office, please. Meanwhile, arrange for Bronte to be admitted, half-hourly neuro obs. And put a rush on the blood test, would you?'

Melanie flicked him a dry look. 'Twenty minutes soon enough for you?'

'Perfect. By then we should know what we're dealing with.'

They held a case conference about an hour later.

'Bronte's come around,' Melanie said, 'and she's stabilising. I've told Mrs Miller she can stay with her in the ward.'

Nick seemed to look through her, blink, then gather himself. 'Sorry. I have a lunch date with the board. They've invited me to the golf club so we'll make this fast, if you don't mind.'

Nice for some, Melanie thought, and felt a bit piqued. She'd hoped they could have gone to the park…

'The blood test confirms our suspicions.' Nick leaned forward and placed his hands on the desktop. 'According to Mrs Miller, she'd allowed Bronte to have charge of her own medication. Wanted her to feel responsible. It's obvious now that the kid was ditching the tablets. Her mother's pretty shocked.'

Melanie raised her eyes to his. 'Perhaps they'd both benefit from some family counselling. I'll have a chat with them about a camp for Bronte as well. I think there's one happening during the next school holidays. She obviously needs the support of other youngsters who have to follow the same kind of health regimen.'

'Oh, good. I'll leave it to you, then.' Nick was dismissive, already on his feet and reaching for his jacket.

Taking her cue from him, Melanie rose too. 'Better not keep the brass waiting, then?'

'Ah...no. Catch you later.' He hardly looked at her, holding the door open barely long enough for her to scramble through.

If you're lucky, Dr Cavallo, Melanie thought crossly, watching him sprint for the car park. She made her way to the staffroom and a chink of humour lifted her spirits. At least Sean would appreciate the extra sandwiches she'd packed.

Melanie hardly touched her lunch at all. Just after Nick had left she received a phone call. She was pale and shaken when she replaced the receiver. For the rest of the afternoon her stomach felt as if it were on a never-ending roller-coaster ride.

She was in her office, her head buried in hated paperwork, when Nick arrived back at the hospital.

'Rather a long lunch, wasn't it, doctor?' she asked primly, glancing pointedly at her fob watch. Keep it light, she told herself, and you just might make it through today without having to tell him anything…

Nick laughed, wandering in and propping himself on the edge of her desk. 'I have something to tell you.'

Melanie's heart fluttered. He looked as pleased as Punch. She put her pen down and waited.

'My place after work?' He walked his fingers playfully across the desk to her arm. 'I'll make you dinner.'

If only she could. 'Nick, I can't come to dinner. I already have a dinner date.' She stopped and bit her lip. Perhaps, after all, it was better to have everything out in the open.

'Oh…' His eyes suddenly raked her face. 'Anyone I know?'

'No.' She took a deep breath and plunged on. 'Aaron Prescott, my—'

'I know who he is, Melanie.' Nick overrode her with an impatient edge to his voice. 'I gather he's in town?'

She nodded. 'He's making a docu-drama about a child who went missing in the district about twenty years ago—'

'Get to the point, Melanie.'

She lowered her gaze, choosing her words as if each one cost a thousand dollars. 'He rang earlier. He wants to see me.'

Nick went very still, all his energies reined in.

'Does he want you back?'

'Don't be ridiculous!' A flood of colour washed over her cheeks. 'He wants to *talk*. And you said yourself, Nick, I should have been more open with him before the marriage ended.'

'That was then.' He stood abruptly and moved to the window, his back to her, stiff and uncommunicative.

Melanie sank her head onto her upturned hand. Telling him had been far worse than she'd imagined. All right, he was feeling vulnerable. Well, so was she, and it was like cutting her heart out.

'If you should decide you want to go back to him...'

Her lashes flickered up. 'What?'

He was facing her, his expression unreadable. 'If you do,' he said deliberately, 'tell me face to face, will you? I don't want a phone call from some flaming airport.'

Melanie was appalled. Was that how he'd learned that Sonia was going back to her former husband?

Oh, dear God...

It was only when he'd gone, closing the door quietly behind him, that Melanie realised he hadn't told her his news.

Next morning she dragged herself to work, thanking heaven it was Friday. She took report and began organising her staff for the day ahead. Nick barely looked at her, wishing her a curt good morning, before shutting himself in his office.

Melanie felt the sharp pain of rejection. It was quite obvious he didn't want to know anything about her meeting with Aaron. Well, she wasn't about to force-feed him the details!

By ten o'clock she felt she was going crazy. Things were unusually quiet and time hung heavily, like a yoke across her shoulders. As for her nurses, with time on their hands they were positively skittish. Smiling a bit grimly, Melanie toyed with the idea of setting them to work carbolising beds. But only for a second. Why make their young lives as miserable as hers was at the moment?

She managed to fill in another half-hour, and then a flurry of squeals, oohs and aahs sent her, a bit tight-lipped, towards Reception. Enough was enough! The place was rapidly turning into a fun-fair.

'Oh, Melanie—look!' Jeannie, the receptionist, Fiona, Jane and Suzy—who was back with them—all crowded around.

Melanie's eyes nearly popped out of her head. Suzy was holding out a bouquet of the most heavenly tulips.

'For me?' They were her very favourite flower.

Nick? For a moment her spirits soared—and then plummeted. These rare, exquisite blooms had certainly not come from the local florist's shop. So where had they come from?

'A courier van brought them from the airport,' Jeannie supplied helpfully. 'Obviously they've been air-freighted from Brisbane.'

'Aren't you going to read the card?' Four pairs of eyes watched expectantly.

A bit dazedly Melanie satisfied their curiosity and then took the flowers to the utility room. She'd need two vases at least, she thought, placing the tulips on the bench. Carefully, she began to undo the Cellophane.

'What's this, then?'

Nick was right behind her but, hurt by his earlier rebuff, she feigned indifference.

'I beg your pardon?'

'Going for the big guns, is he?'

She met Nick's eyes, startled. He thought the flowers were from Aaron...

'Nick, it's not what you think.'

His mouth grew taut. 'I understood you were only going to talk.'

Stunned, Melanie spun to face him. 'That's all we did, for heaven's sake!'

'I'll bet!' he said under his breath. 'Pull the other leg, Melanie. It yodels!'

Melanie's anger kept her going until lunchtime. Then she decided how ridiculous it all was. She'd make Nick listen even if she had to tie him to a chair.

She searched the length and breadth of the A and E department and couldn't find him, finally tapping on his office door. When there was no response she cautiously opened it and peered in. The room was ominously empty.

Premonition clutched at her and made her uneasy. Someone must know something. She confronted a startled Sean across a treatment trolley.

'Could I have a word, please, Dr Casey?'

'Won't be a tick,' Sean said to his patient, whose treatment he'd just completed anyway, and followed Melanie outside.

'Where's Nick?' she asked, without preamble.

Sean peered at his watch and pointed upwards.

'Airborne by now, I should think.'

'What?'

'He didn't tell you?'

Now that was the understatement of the year. She shook her head.

'He arranged cover for the weekend and took off. Literally,' Sean said. 'Caught the noon plane.'

'I'm working a late shift tomorrow,' Melanie told Tam as they drove home together that afternoon.

Tam twitched an eyebrow. 'You never work weekends. How come?'

Melanie shrugged. 'Favour for Mike Treloar. Chris is being discharged from hospital tomorrow morning. Naturally, Mike wants to be there.'

'Well, nice for them,' Tam said practically, 'but what about your plans? Weren't you and Nick hoping to go on a picnic? Does he mind?'

Melanie gave a cracked laugh. 'I don't know what Nick thinks. He's taken himself off somewhere. Back Monday, apparently.'

Melanie recounted the story briefly.

'Good grief!' Tam said softly. 'Men are the absolute pits sometimes.'

CHAPTER TWELVE

Now I know why I gave up working on weekends, Melanie reminded herself ruefully. The shift was short-staffed and busy. And she'd forgotten that winter also meant football injuries.

In the staffroom she swallowed a quickly made cup of tea and glanced at her watch. Four hours down and four to go. Please, God, let them be quiet.

It seemed her prayer was not about to be answered. The sound of a disturbance sent her hurrying back out to Reception. What on earth was going on? Melanie could hardly believe her eyes.

A huge man in what looked like biker's leathers was systematically thumping open the doors to every room.

'I tried to stop him...' A junior nurse shrank back against the wall where the man had obviously pushed her.

'Ring Security,' Melanie ordered, a prickle of alarm teasing the back of her neck. Here was trouble and most of the male staff were on a meal break.

Terrific!

'What do you think you're doing?' Moving swiftly, Melanie effectively blocked the man's way to the treatment room.

'You mob've got my girlfriend here and I want

her out.' The smell of alcohol curled off the man's breath in nauseating waves, and Melanie reeled back.

'I told her not to come here, telling tales. I told her!' His fist slammed into the wall, missing Melanie's cheek by barely a centimetre.

'She's not here.' Melanie strove for calm and authority. 'And you shouldn't be here, either. You're trespassing.'

'She is here! You lying bitch!' The man lifted a fist threateningly. 'Get outa my way.'

Melanie felt the jarring crunch and gave a cry of pain as the intruder's beefy hands caught her by the shoulders. Her slight body was no match for his brute strength, and she was yanked roughly away from the door and shoved backwards along the corridor.

She gave a gasp, feeling herself falling, falling and then caught. Hard. Against a trolley?

In a haze of terror she realised that whatever had broken her fall was no hospital trolley. It had human form. Dear heaven—were there two of them?

Fear whimpered out of her throat, ending in a choking sob.

'I've got you... I've got you...'

The words echoed and spun through her head, then she was turned into protective arms and held. Safe.

She heard running feet and raised voices. But above them all one voice took charge.

'Call the police!'

'I've called Security, Dr Cavallo.'

'Call the police!' Nick roared. 'I want him charged.'

Melanie felt the muscles in his arms tense. 'Let's

get out of here,' he rasped. Shielding her from the ugly scene, he led her to his office and kicked the door shut.

'Nick, I'm all right,' she said quickly. 'Just scared half to death.' His hard, searching look told her he didn't quite believe her.

'Does it hurt anywhere?'

She stared at him bemusedly as he gently peeled back her uniform and examined the skin around her shoulders and collar-bone. She bit her lip. His clothes were creased and his face was shadowed with beard, but he'd never looked more wonderful, more desirable.

'You might have a bruise there tomorrow,' he said. 'Don't ever do anything like that again, Melanie.' He was speaking softly, curving her back into his arms.

Melanie offered no resistance as his hands continued to move over her body. He raised her head briefly to look down at her. 'I think I lost ten years off my life, watching you out there. I love you!' The words were wrung from him, and his mouth made feathery kisses over her temple, her eyes, cheek and back to her mouth, his possession fiercely brief.

'Do you love me?' His voice shook.

'Of course I love you. Of course—'

Her words were blotted out by his kiss, and she responded with a wildness that matched his own, filled with a need to be part of him, to hold him and have him hold her. For ever.

They went home to Crafters.

Showered and dressed in towelling robes, they sat

closely together on the old chesterfield. Nick had lit the fire and poured them both a small whisky.

'Where've you been?' Melanie took a mouthful of her drink and made a face.

'Walking.'

'Since noon yesterday?'

He shrugged. 'I got the plane to Brisbane and hired a car. I drove down to the coast. Walked for hours along the beach.' He stopped and downed half the contents of his glass. 'I finally decided that if I loved you I'd better damn well get back here and fight for you.'

Melanie's mouth curved wryly. 'Well you almost did that.'

Nick glowered. 'I meant What's-his-name.'

'Aaron,' Melanie said clearly. 'Nick, we talked, that's all. And it was good. Cleansing, I suppose.' She stared into her whisky. 'He's no threat to you, Nick. He never was.'

His mouth tightened. 'Thank you for telling me.'

He gave a huff of raw laughter. 'I was under the impression that being in love was supposed to make you happy. But for the last twenty-four hours my insides have felt as though a very bad surgeon had been let loose on me.'

A tiny throb of joy was starting at the back of Melanie's head. It was like a muted waterfall, echoing the wild, hopeful lilt of her heart.

'I want to meet your parents,' Nick said in an abrupt change of mood. 'How soon can we get down to Sydney?'

Melanie blinked, confused.

'It's time this family started pulling together,' he said. 'I want our kids to know their grandparents, don't you?'

It was all too much. All she'd dreamed of was happening. Her throat began tightening in painful spasms. 'Are you asking me to marry you, Nick?'

'Yes, Mel.' Nick's voice was gentle. 'If you'll have me.'

With a little shiver, which had nothing to do with atmospheric conditions, she ran her palms down his lean cheeks, halted and dragged in a deep breath.

'Yes, Nick. I'll have you.'

'Oh, boy!'

She hiccuped a laugh and they kissed breathlessly.

'Who were the tulips from?' Nick murmured when they came up for air.

'I don't think I'll tell you.' She tilted her head, saw the naked vulnerability in his eyes and relented.

'They were from Kiyo and her husband. Sent through Interflora. And she's pregnant again.'

'Good grief!' Nick growled. 'Doesn't anyone listen to their doctor? I told her to go slow for a bit. At least I thought I had.'

Melanie's laughter bubbled up. 'Well, her interpretation of English was a bit mixed. Maybe she thought you said "go for it".' She burrowed closer. 'You never did tell me your news. After you met the board.'

'Ah...'

'What did they say?' she prompted. 'Was it to thank you and give you a reference?'

'Not exactly.'

Startled by the tone of his voice, she turned to look at him. 'No?'

He shrugged. 'They've offered me a further contract. A year this time. Maybe an option for longer. They've secured funding for another general surgeon.'

She swallowed, hardly daring to believe what she was hearing. And hoping. 'You'd want to get back to one of the big hospitals, though, wouldn't you?'

Nick intertwined their hands and curled them over his heart. 'I've found what I want right here.'

She looked into his eyes with hers alight with love, excitement and plain wonderment. 'You mean, we could get married and live here in the cottage?'

'For a while at least,' Nick said. 'If it's what you want, too.'

'Oh, Nick. That's perfect!'

'Like you.' He linked his arms more comfortably around her. 'It's remarkable how we both ended up in Murrajong, isn't it?'

'It was kismet, surely?' Melanie snuggled against him, her mind busy with plans for their shared life to come. Such plans...'

'Just had a thought.' Nick turned his vivid blue gaze to her.

'Mmm?'

'By the time we're ready to leave Murrajong we might be three. Or four...' He grinned down at her, a carefree, youthfully happy grin.

Melanie grinned back. He was reading her mind again.

MILLS & BOON®

Makes any time special

Enjoy a romantic novel from
Mills & Boon®

Presents™ *Enchanted*™ *Temptation*

Historical Romance™ *Medical Romance*™

MILLS & BOON®

Medical Romance™

COMING NEXT MONTH

All these books are especially for Mother's Day

✱   ✱   ✱

A HERO FOR MOMMY by Jessica Matthews

Dr Ben Shepherd was unprepared for the impact Kelly Evers and her five-year-old daughter Carlie would have on his life...

BE MY MUMMY by Josie Metcalfe

Jack Madison's small son Danny was a delight, and he and Lauren were very drawn to each other. But why does this make Jack edgy?

MUM'S THE WORD by Alison Roberts

Dr Sarah Kendall anticipated a happy family life when she accepted Paul's proposal, but Paul's son Daniel had other ideas!

WANTED: A MOTHER by Elisabeth Scott

Adam Kerr needed a live-in nurse for his ten-year-old daughter Jeannie, but Meg Bennett was *so* much younger and prettier than he expected...

Available from 5th March 1999

Available at most branches of WH Smith, Tesco, Asda, Martins, Borders, Easons, Volume One/James Thin and most good paperback bookshops

MILLS & BOON®

Next Month's Romance Titles

♡

Each month you can choose from a wide variety of romance novels from Mills & Boon®. Below are the new titles to look out for next month from the Presents™ and Enchanted™ series.

Presents™

THE MARRIAGE DECIDER	Emma Darcy
TO BE A BRIDEGROOM	Carole Mortimer
HOT SURRENDER	Charlotte Lamb
THE BABY SECRET	Helen Brooks
A HUSBAND'S VENDETTA	Sara Wood
BABY DOWN UNDER	Ann Charlton
A RECKLESS SEDUCTION	Jayne Bauling
OCCUPATION: MILLIONAIRE	Alexandra Sellers

Enchanted™

A WEDDING WORTH WAITING FOR	Jessica Steele
CAROLINE'S CHILD	Debbie Macomber
SLEEPLESS NIGHTS	Anne Weale
ONE BRIDE DELIVERED	Jeanne Allan
A FUNNY THING HAPPENED…	Caroline Anderson
HAND-PICKED HUSBAND	Heather MacAllister
A MOST DETERMINED BACHELOR	Miriam Macgregor
INTRODUCING DADDY	Alaina Hawthorne

On sale from 5th March 1999

H1 9902

Available at most branches of WH Smith, Tesco, Asda, Martins, Borders, Easons, Volume One/James Thin and most good paperback bookshops

MILLS & BOON®

Makes any time special™

By Request

Bestselling themed romances brought back to you by popular demand

Each month By Request brings you three full-length novels in one beautiful volume featuring the best of the best.

So if you missed a favourite Romance the first time around, here is your chance to relive the magic from some of our most popular authors.

Look out for
Conveniently Yours **in February 1999 featuring Emma Darcy, Helen Bianchin and Michelle Reid**

Available at most branches of WH Smith, Tesco, Asda, Martins, Borders, Easons, Volume One/James Thin and most good paperback bookshops

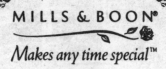

MILLS & BOON®

Makes any time special™

By Request

Bestselling themed romances brought back to you by popular demand

Each month By Request brings you three full-length novels in one beautiful volume featuring the best of the best.

So if you missed a favourite Romance the first time around, here is your chance to relive the magic from some of our most popular authors.

Look out for
***Sole Paternity* in March 1999**
featuring Miranda Lee, Robyn Donald
and Sandra Marton

Available at most branches of WH Smith, Tesco, Asda, Martins, Borders, Easons, Volume One/James Thin and most good paperback bookshops

FREE!

2 Books

and a surprise gift!

We would like to take this opportunity to thank you for reading this Mills & Boon® book by offering you the chance to take TWO more specially selected titles from the Medical Romance™ series absolutely FREE! We're also making this offer to introduce you to the benefits of the Reader Service™—

- ★ FREE home delivery
- ★ FREE gifts and competitions
- ★ FREE monthly Newsletter
- ★ Books available before they're in the shops
- ★ Exclusive Reader Service discounts

Accepting these FREE books and gift places you under no obligation to buy; you may cancel at any time, even after receiving your free shipment. Simply complete your details below and return the entire page to the address below. *You don't even need a stamp!*

YES! Please send me 2 free Medical Romance books and a surprise gift. I understand that unless you hear from me, I will receive 4 superb new titles every month for just £2.40 each, postage and packing free. I am under no obligation to purchase any books and may cancel my subscription at any time. The free books and gift will be mine to keep in any case.

M9EB

Ms/Mrs/Miss/Mr ....Initials ....
BLOCK CAPITALS PLEASE

Surname ....

Address...

....

....Postcode ....

Send this whole page to:
THE READER SERVICE, FREEPOST CN81, CROYDON, CR9 3WZ
(Eire readers please send coupon to: P.O. Box 4546, DUBLIN 24.)

Offer not valid to current Reader Service subscribers to this series. We reserve the right to refuse an application and applicants must be aged 18 years or over. Only one application per household. Terms and prices subject to change without notice. Offer expires 31st August 1999. As a result of this application, you may receive further offers from Harlequin Mills & Boon and other carefully selected companies. If you would prefer not to share in this opportunity please write to The Data Manager at the address above.

Medical Romance is a registered trademark owned by Harlequin Mills & Boon Limited.

DIANA PALMER

ONCE in PARIS

Brianne Martin rescued grief-stricken Pierce
Hutton from the depths of despair, but before
she knew it, Brianne had become a pawn in an
international web of deceit and corruption.
Now it was Pierce's turn to rescue Brianne.
What had they stumbled into?
They would be lucky to escape with their lives!

1-55166-470-4

MIRA® Available in paperback from March, 1999